Daddy's Rules

KELLY MYERS

Copyright © 2021

All rights reserved. No part of this publication may be reproduced, distributed, or transmitted in any form or by any means, including photocopying, recording, or other electronic or mechanical methods, without the prior written permission of the publisher, except in the case of brief quotations embodied in critical reviews and certain other non-commercial uses permitted by copyright law.

This is a work of fiction. While, as in all fiction, the literary perceptions and insights are based on life experiences and conclusions drawn from research, all names, characters, places and specific instances are products of the author's imagination and used fictitiously. No actual reference to any real person, living or dead, is intended or inferred.

Blurb

He's always surrounded by gorgeous women.
Models.
Supermodels.

And one of his three important rules?
Never mix business with pleasure.

Nick is the best photographer in Hollywood.
He's older, always in control, and oh-so-tempting.
Being in Vegas with Nick as his model did a number on me.
We ended up having way too much fun.
One kiss led to another and the next thing I know?
I've got a ring on my finger and tears in my eyes.
Nick doesn't get emotionally involved.
That's another one of his rules.
If he falls for me, he'd be breaking two of his three rules.

The third one is to never let me take control in bed.
That's the only one I like.

But what if I end up pregnant?
Would that make him break the other two rules?
And if he doesn't, then it's my heart he'll be breaking...

Chapter One: Savannah

When I get the call that everyone says will change my life, I hope it's true. Something deep down in my gut, in my heart, knows that things are about to change in a big way for me, but it's definitely not what I'm expecting.

Or, should I say not *whom* I'm expecting.

I may be a small town girl from Ohio, but I have always had big dreams. Growing up, people constantly told me I should be a model. Probably because I look like a scarecrow-- tall and skinny with long blonde hair. It took me a while to grow into my gangly self and, half the time, I still think that I resemble a long-legged baby deer more often than not. But, now at 21, I know my angles, my proportions and how best to use the light to highlight my attributes.

A few modeling classes helped and binge-watching America's Next Top Model taught me a lot. But, I've learned you either have it or you don't when it comes to modeling. You don't have to be the prettiest or the tallest or the skinniest to book an important gig. What you need, the thing that all supermodels have, is that certain *je ne sais quoi*. And, it can't be taught or bought or learned.

I've been told I have it. They say when the camera starts clicking, I sparkle.

I'm not sure about that, but I do know that when the photographer starts taking pictures, I go to another place. My body goes on autopilot and somehow knows exactly what to do. It's almost like an out of body experience and I can see myself posing, and I just go with the flow and let it all happen naturally.

So, when my agent calls and tells me that I just booked a once-in-a-lifetime campaign with Guess, I'm thrilled. I've been working toward this moment since I was 15 and it's taken me six years. I'm extremely grateful because I know that a model has a short shelf-life. Normally, if you don't make it by 21, you're done.

I made it.

The paycheck that comes with this type of campaign is the whole reason I decided to pursue modeling in the first place. I have no desire to design fragrances or start a clothing line or transition into acting when my modeling days are over at the ripe old age of 25. Instead, I'm going to save every penny I earn and put it toward school and opening my own practice.

I've always loved animals and my real dream is to become a veterinarian. Modeling will just be the way I finance that dream.

While most girls my age are busy partying and dating, I pretty much avoid all that and stay focused on the big picture. I don't have time to go out and get drunk and date random guys when I have a photoshoot at 6am the next morning. That means being on set and ready to shoot at that exact time, not wandering in the door with a coffee. Hair, wardrobe and makeup can take anywhere from two to three hours. So, a 6am call time more than likely means that my butt needs to be there by 3am.

It's never been a problem for me. My parents taught me to respect other people and their time. I was raised to have a good work ethic and, even if I am the headliner or star or whatever you want to call it, I wouldn't have a job if I didn't work hard and do my best.

No matter how talented you may be, people don't want to work with an asshole. So, I always make sure I am considerate, professional and kind to everyone I encounter whether it's the hotshot photographer or the craft service person.

I wonder who the photographer on the campaign will be? I've worked with some amazing and talented ones and I'm sure this time will be no exception. As my excitement starts to build, I decide to call home and share the news.

My mom answers in her usual cheery, upbeat voice. "Hi, Savannah. I was just going to call you."

Bob and Cindy Hart, my parents, had me and my younger sister Bri when they were well into their 40s. Now, they're both retired school teachers and still as happy and in love as the day they got married. I've been lucky to have such a good example of love and, maybe one day, after I'm a successful vet, I'll meet the man of my dreams.

Currently, though, I'm in no rush.

"Hi, Mom. I have some big news," I tell her in a sing-song voice.

"You booked the campaign?"

I can hear the excitement in her voice and I squeal. "I am officially a Guess Girl."

"Oh, honey, I'm so proud of you," she gushes. "Hold on, I have to tell your father."

I laugh as my Mom shares the good news. "Is Bri there?" I ask.

"No, she's at a birthday party with some friends."

Of course, she is, I think. My 16-year old sister is a social butterfly. Way more outgoing than me and always in the thick of things. I think she's been class president twice, a cheerleader for both the basketball and football teams and on the Homecoming Court as a freshman which is practically unheard of at our high school. It means she'll be a shoe-in for Queen one day.

"Okay, well, tell her to call me."

"I will. Where's your shoot taking place?"

"Las Vegas." I've never been to Sin City so it should be interesting. I just turned 21 last month so it's the perfect time now that I'm legal. I can drink, gamble and go to all the hottest clubs. *Yeah, right. Who am I kidding?* I'm going to be tucked away in my room, probably pampering myself, resting up and ordering room service.

Same routine, different city. I don't vary too much from the usual get-lots-of-rest before a photo shoot. I refuse to stumble on set after a night of partying with dark circles under my blue eyes and a bloated face and stomach from too much alcohol.

Not that I'd really know, though. Other than a sip here or there, I don't drink. And, unlike my extrovert sister, I don't remember the last party I attended.

You are boring and predictable, Savvy.

I talk to my Mom for a bit longer and then hang up. For some reason, my thoughts keep returning to the fact that I recently turned 21 and didn't celebrate. I was working that day and didn't even eat the cupcake my neighbor Jasmine gave me. I don't really regret it, but, at the same time, I wonder if something is wrong with me. *Am I too serious? Too focused? Should I let loose a little bit?*

Jasmine Torres is a few years older than me and a model, too. She mostly does runway and she's striking with long, silky black hair and dark almond-shaped eyes. Her exotic beauty is the complete opposite of my All-American blonde hair and blue eyes.

I'd love to look like Jasmine and have her confidence. She's originally from Texas and, even though she's only 25, she has this motherly quality toward all the younger girls who live here at Sunset Terrace. She always has some kind of wisdom to share and manages to slip a "y'all" in every other sentence.

Sunset Terrace, my apartment complex, consists of 12 units and a crystal blue pool in the middle where we like to hang out on our days off. It's all very Melrose Place looking and my neighbors, like me, are here in Hollywood to pursue their dreams.

Jasmine and I are the models and have had the most success. Taylor, my other neighbor, is a dancer. She studies ballet during the day and is freaking amazing. The way she can twirl and dip blows my mind and she has this natural grace and elegance that makes me feel like a clutz. And, even though being a classically-trained ballerina is her dream, she can drop it like it's hot and hit the dance floor like she was born to be a hip hop dancer. To pay the bills, she dances at night at a nearby club and is always inviting us down there.

I keep telling myself, and her, that I'll go. I just haven't had the time or inclination yet.

Our friend Morgan lives a few apartments over and she's the only one of us actually from SoCal. She's been trying to break into acting for quite awhile now and her Mom is really sick with cancer. I feel bad for her and know that she works extra shifts as a cocktail waitress to help pay her Mom's hospital bills. I see how tired she looks sometimes and can see her dream starting to fade away and reality setting in. I'm not sure how much longer she's going to be able to go out on auditions and keep getting rejected. Acting is a brutal industry and I wouldn't wish it on anyone. Even if you're talented, your chances of making it are slim to none.

In Hollywood, when it comes to making movies, it's all who you know.

And, poor Morgan doesn't know anyone.

A few of the residents here keep to themselves, but the group of us in our 20s have bonded and like to hang out and talk about how we're going to take this town by storm and make it big. There are a couple of cute guys, but no one I'm interested in pursuing. Twenty-something guys are really just boys, in my opinion. All they want to do is get drunk and have sex.

When I first moved into the complex last year, my upstairs neighbor Mason asked me out, but I politely declined. He lives with Cody and they're such typical frat boys. Constantly drinking, partying and hooking up.

Bleh.

I think when I decide to start looking for a significant other, he's going to be older. I need a man who is mature, dependable and considerate. Someone who will take their time and be patient and not rush me into anything. Especially sex.

I've put it off this long so when I finally sleep with a man, I want it to be a *man*. To me, a real man is someone who will move slowly and teach me things that I don't know. And, let's face it, I don't know much. When I was 12, I was still playing with Barbies and nowadays, there are 12-year olds who are pregnant.

It kind of blows my mind, but I try not to judge. To each his own, right?

Hmm. Then, it occurs to me that maybe I'm the one who's missing out. Am I letting my best years slip by me because I'm too busy planning my future?

No, I decide, and reach into my fridge and pull out a pop. As I take a sip, I know that I could've stayed in Ohio and led a normal life. I could be married by now with a kid on the way. But, I wanted more. And, one of these days, I'll go back home, open up my practice and maybe find a nice man to settle down with.

But, for now, I'm going to work my butt off, save money and hope that this campaign with Guess will launch my career into the stratosphere.

Then, maybe I'll take a quick break and pop open a bottle of champagne with my neighbors.

Maybe.

Chapter Two: Nick

Maybe I should just fucking marry her, I think.

I let out a breath and run a frustrated hand through my dark hair. Problem is, Margo York is giving me an ultimatum and I don't like that. She's backed me into a corner and is now demanding that I propose marriage or we break up.

How romantic.

Sure, we've been dating for a year, but what the hell is the rush? And, when I ask her that, she gets even more pissed. I seriously can't win.

"Nick," she snaps and I force myself to look back over into her pale green eyes. She crosses her arms and taps the empty ring finger on her left hand as though reminding me there should be a sparkling diamond there. "If you don't want to marry me then what are we even doing? Because it feels like you're just wasting my time."

When it comes to women, I have three rules: 1. Never get emotionally-involved. Keep it purely physical. That doesn't mean I can't develop a modicum of affection for her. I'm not a robot, for chrissake. But, when all is said and done, love is for suckers and it's important to be able to walk away, if need be, and not look back.

My second rule: Never let her take control in bed. I'm in charge and she doesn't come until I say. This doesn't mean she can't initiate sex. Sometimes that turns me on, knowing that she desires me. But, when it comes down to it, I'm the man, the alpha, and I call the shots.

And, lastly, my third rule: Never mix business with pleasure. This is the most important one because I'm a photographer and my job requires me to work closely with models. Young, beautiful, empty-headed girls who will do anything to make it in this Industry. But, if they try to cross the line, I will ignore their advances because the last thing I want is a sleazy reputation or sexual allegations or charges against me when they decide they aren't happy with the shoot or something I said pissed them off. #MeToo is taking down quite a few power players and I want nothing to do with that shit. I am a professional with a sterling rep and I plan to keep it that way.

Right now, Margo is a perfect example of why I have rule number one. Even though we've been together for about a year, though on and off, I am not attached to her. I can kick her out of my life and my bed right now without blinking.

Maybe that makes me cold, but I think it's smart. Heartbreak is a horrible thing and I don't ever want to set myself up to potentially experience it. I saw firsthand how it broke my Mom when my Dad left her. It took her years to pick up the broken pieces and get her life back together. Now, she's with John, my stepdad, who is a good and kind man who treats her with the respect she deserves.

But, what if he had never come along? I think she'd still be curled up in bed, crying her eyes out over a man who never gave a shit about her or me.

Fuck that.

I have a bit of a dilemma, though. As much as I want to tell Margo to walk, there's something she doesn't know. She thinks I'm pretty well-off financially, but that's hardly the case. The truth is I'm drowning in debt. Mostly because of her.

Here's the catch, though. My eccentric Grandmother died last year and, since I was her only grandchild, she left me a nice-sized inheritance around $200 grand. Problem is, there's just one stipulation. I don't get a dime until I get married.

So, I can marry Margo and roll in the dough. Or, retain my sanity and debt and break up with her.

Margo York has me by the balls and doesn't even know it.

Money never concerned Margo because she's a trust fund baby who spends her days shopping, doing yoga and meeting her wealthy girlfriends for lunch. Her biggest concern is usually a chipped nail. Her family is worth around half a billion, old money, and I think her great-grandpa was a first-class passenger on the Titanic. Shit, if his wife was anything like Margo, he probably chose to go down with the ship.

I'm not going to lie. She's my meal ticket, the answer to my current financial problems. But, hell, the majority of my debt is due to her. Even though she's loaded, Margo expects me to pay for everything. And, I don't mind that, but, at the same time, when we have to go to the most expensive restaurants for dinner, fly first class, take exotic vacations and stay in 5-star resorts, the great money I make as a fashion photographer disappears quicker than a virgin on prom night.

And, now she wants a ring?

Christ, help me.

I can only imagine how much that would cost because if I know Margo, she's already picked the ring out and it probably costs a fortune. I can already hear her whining: *"But, Nicky, I have to have it. Yellow diamonds are all the rage now so I can't very well have a plain, boring, clear diamond."*

God fucking forbid.

I feel a headache begin to pound behind my eyes and I just want her to leave. All I want is a quiet night with a couple beers and some In-N-Out burger. Or, better yet, a nice greasy pizza.

Margo would probably rather die than consume fast food. And, beer? Well, that's the poor man's drink. Margo only sips $30 martinis. Half the time, she doesn't even finish them. *"I just want to try a sip, Nicky," she says and orders three.*

I can't support her lavish lifestyle any longer and I'm drowning in debt, but she doesn't seem to notice or care. If I marry her, though, *her* money becomes *our* money. Right?

And, then there's the inheritance that I'll finally be able to get my hands on.

So, do I marry her and be debt-free and miserable? Or, do I break it off and just fucking declare bankruptcy?

I grit my jaw hard, not liking either choice.

"You're not even paying attention to me. I can't do this anymore," Margo yells. I blink back to attention and see her snatch her designer handbag up off a chair and storm toward the front door. She grabs the handle and glances over her shoulder. "You have one week to make a decision, Nicholas. Either propose or it's over."

She slams the door behind her and I roll my eyes. As I massage my temples with my fingertips, I try not to think too hard about her threat. Here's the thing-- I may be 42, but I am not ready to get married yet. At least not to Margo York.

God, I used to have more money than I knew what to do with. In my 20s, I was a top male model and walked the runways in Europe and did campaigns for designers like Versace, Dolce & Gabbana and Ralph Lauren. I bought this beach house in Malibu and dumped my Toyota for my dream car-- a Dodge Demon which is a limited piece of automotive history. With 840 horsepower, she can do 0-60 miles per hour in 2.3 seconds and 0-30 mph in a second flat. Driving that baby down the Pacific Coast Highway is better than fucking a supermodel.

Trust me, I know. I've had my fair share and despite their beauty, most are vapid, boring and have zero personality.

For me, modeling held no challenge and I found myself becoming more and more interested in photògraphy. One day, I bought a camera and started taking pictures. And, they were damn good. I discovered a talent I never knew I had and began booking gigs on the other end of the lens.

Along the way, I guess I became a little...arrogant. I knew my pictures were better than the majority out there and I knew how to get a good shot fast. But, at some point, my reputation turned from exciting new photographer to moody and difficult to work with.

And, now, when I need money, the photography jobs have dried up.

I don't think I should apologize for having high standards, though. I expect my crew and the talent to work hard. If they slack or don't take the job seriously, I'm going to get pissed. What's so wrong with that?

On my set, I maintain a professional atmosphere at all times and I challenge everyone around me to rise to the occasion. Not to be better, but to be the best. I won't tolerate anything but perfection.

Apparently, my brilliance at getting phenomenal pictures is the reason I have a difficult reputation. *It's bullshit.* An artist is under a lot of pressure to succeed and most people don't have a clue what it takes to make it in this town.

Now that Margo is gone, I head into the kitchen and grab a beer out of the fridge. I think I'll order that pizza, too, I decide. With extra pepperoni, bacon and sausage.

"Processed meats are full of nitrates and nitrites, Nicholas," she would say in that silky voice of hers. *"But, if you want to get cancer then go right ahead and order it."*

I pick up the phone and place the order.

Then, I wander outside, onto the back deck, and lean against the wooden rail, eyes on the gray waves of the Pacific Ocean. It's still overcast today, but the end of June Gloom is in sight since July is almost here. I don't mind the cooler weather and mistiness but, after a month, I'm ready for vibrant blue skies and the warm sun again.

As I take another sip of the beer, my phone rings. It's my agent and I answer on the second ring. "Nick Knight," I say.

"Nick, it's Deirdre. What are you doing this weekend? Because I have an amazing job opportunity for you."

"What's the job?" I ask, interest piqued.

"Guess campaign with a new up and coming model. It's going to be brilliant and guarantee a hefty paycheck for you. The shoot is Saturday and Sunday, but we'll fly you in a day early to get situated."

"Where?"

"Las Vegas, baby. After the shoot, you can stay a day or two and get some gambling in if you want. What do you say, Nick?"

"Who's the model?" I ask.

I hear some shuffling and wait while she tries to find the newbie's name. "Uh, Sierra, no, wait, Savannah. Savannah Hart."

Never heard of her. But, all it takes is one campaign like this to launch a model's career. And, I like that kind of challenge. And, God knows, I could also use the paycheck. There's a stack of bills on the kitchen counter and I've been dreading opening them for over a week now.

"Book it," I say. Even if this Savannah Hart never modeled a day in her life and looks like a toad, I have the talent and expertise to make her look like a million bucks. Like a superstar. And, even though the money won't solve my current dilemma, it will help.

Vegas, here I come.

Chapter Three: Savannah

When I find out the photographer I'm going to be working with is Nick Knight, I'm not sure how to feel. I've heard a few rumors that he's an arrogant ass so I decide to invite my neighbor Jasmine over and get the scoop while I pack.

Jasmine Torres leans back on my bed and crosses her long, long tan legs. "Nick Knight is a brilliant photographer," she assures me. "But, he can also be difficult and demanding."

"Should I be nervous?" I ask.

"No. I think he only gets pissy when people act unprofessional and waste his time."

"Well, that's understandable."

"And, you're a total pro on set so don't even worry about it. I'm sure y'all will get along just fine."

I toss some leggings into the suitcase and then look up with a smile. "I'm so excited, Jazz. This is the biggest thing I've ever booked. And, the paycheck…" I shake my head, still in disbelief. "I can't believe how much money it is!"

"Welcome to the big leagues, baby! We're going to have to take a trip to New York and go see your billboard in Times Square."

"Oh, my gosh, can you imagine?" We both squeal. "So, when did you work with Nick?" I ask and rummage through my dresser for some pajamas to pack.

She studies her nails, thinking. "Must have been about three years ago. When I did the Marc Jacobs shoot."

"And, he was nice to you?"

She makes a face. "I wouldn't describe Nick Knight as nice," she says carefully. "But, he's very focused and keeps things extremely professional. So, the good thing is you don't have to worry about some sleaze trying to hit on you."

I let out a little breath and nod. "That's a relief. I don't want to deal with some creepy perv all weekend."

With a laugh, Jasmine glances down at what I've packed so far and frowns. "Um, you do realize that you're going to Las Vegas, right?"

"What do you mean?" I frown.

"Savvy, by the looks of what you've packed, I'd guess you're going camping." She pulls out a plaid shirt and cringes. "What is this ridiculousness? You're supposed to be a model and have a little style. This looks like a shirt my Grandpa owns."

"Gimme that." I grab the shirt and toss it back into the suitcase. Okay, so maybe I'm packing practical clothes. What's wrong with that? I'll barely be wearing my own clothes, anyway. When doubt starts to fill my mind, I tilt my head and chew my bottom lip. "What do you think I should bring?" I ask.

If Jasmine is good at anything, it's giving advice.

"You should have at least two or three club outfits, an outfit to wear to the casino, a bathing suit and, for the love of God, Savannah, pack some sexy pajamas."

I look down at the long, pink cotton nightgown in my hands. I suppose it is a little similar to one my Grandma wears. But, I shake my head and frown. "I don't do sexy."

"You don't know *how* to do sexy," she corrects. "But, I can help you. Just because you're a virgin doesn't mean you have to dress like one."

A blush heats my cheeks as she jumps off the bed and starts going through my closet and drawers, pulling things out and tossing them in a pile. Then, she starts matching things up. "Okay, this is about as good as it gets. But, you're lucky I'm such a good friend because I'm going to let you borrow a couple of things. Be right back," she says and jogs out.

While Jasmine runs back to her apartment, I check out the outfits she pieced together and think they're pretty cute. I place them in my suitcase, toss in the shoes she chose and wait for her to return.

When she walks back in, she's holding a hanger with a slinky red dress dangling on it that screams sex. "This little number comes with a hard-on guarantee."

I roll my eyes. "I don't think I want to take it then," I say, but she shoves the dress at me.

"You are definitely taking it. And, I have some pajamas for you," she adds and holds up a sexy little nightgown. It's a powder pink, silk slip edged with lace. "I got to keep it after I walked in the La Perla show. Twelve-hundred dollars, baby. Can you believe it?"

I let out a sigh and tuck the lingerie inside then zip it up. "You act like I'm going to have some kind of secret rendezvous," I say.

She shrugs. "You never know."

I laugh. "Oh, I know. I'm going to be in my room when I'm not working and either reading a book or-"

Jasmine holds up a hand. "Savannah, do me a favor. After your shoot Saturday, go out. Please, please, please wear the red dress, have a glass of champagne and celebrate. Even if it's just you. You're going to be all made up, looking absolutely stunning with big Guess hair, a ton of makeup and probably look just like Claudia Schiffer in the 90s. Take some time and enjoy it, okay?"

Maybe she's right, I think. It wouldn't hurt to do that and just enjoy the moment before going back up to my room and washing the makeup off. "I'll think about it," I say. "Thank you for the dress and sexy nightgown. Even though I have no one to wear it for."

"Never say never," she says with a wink. "Live a little, Savvy. You're going to be in the city of sin. And, I'm going to call you Saturday night and check in. And, I swear to God, if you're sitting in your room by yourself, I'm going to get in my car, drive to Vegas and drag your butt down to the bar."

"Your car's in the shop," I remind her.

"Then, I'll borrow Taylor's car."

"Are you trying to be a bad influence?"

"Who? Me?" she asks all innocently.

I plop down next to her and try to calm my nerves. When I booked this, I knew it was a big deal but now I'm starting to get anxious. What if I mess up? What if I'm off my game? I start to pick at my nail polish and Jasmine bats my hand.

"Anything else I should know about this photographer?" I ask her. "You know I like to be prepared."

"Just that he's hot as sin."

"What?" My head snaps up from my now chipped nail polish. "Are you serious?"

"You've never seen him?"

When I shake my head, she whistles under her breath, grabs her phone and starts typing. "Here he is," she says and turns the screen around to show me a picture of Nick Knight.

Oh. My. Goodness.

I swallow hard and study his perfect features. With high, sharp cheekbones that could cut glass, dark hair and...I zoom in on his eyes and feel my heartbeat quicken...silvery-gray eyes that remind me of liquid metal, Nick Knight is the most attractive man I've ever laid eyes on.

"He used to be a model," she says. "I think he retired like 15 years ago."

"How old is he?" I do a quick search on my phone and see he's 42 years old.

Jasmine shrugs. "Doesn't really matter. I told you-- he's a total professional on set and won't look twice at you. Not in that way. Besides, I'm pretty sure he has a girlfriend."

Of course he does. A guy like that probably has his pick of women. *Boo.*

"Who?" I wonder and scroll through the endless articles about him online.

"Some socialite."

Then, I see her. She looks around his age, maybe 40, and it says her name is Margo York. With sleek, shoulder-length dark hair and pale green eyes, she's rather striking. "Margo York," I mumble.

"That's it! I think she's worth millions."

Good for her, I think and close the app. *I hope they're very happy together.*

Jasmine eyes me then smirks. "I can't believe it."

"What?"

"I never thought I'd see the day."

"What're you talking about?"

"Savannah Hart just found a man she thinks is attractive."

"Oh, shut it," I say. But, when my cheeks redden, there's no denying it. *"What?"* She's staring at me like I have three heads and it's starting to make me mad.

"You are too cute, Savvy."

"He's...very handsome," I admit, feeling flustered. "Anyone with eyes can see that."

"He's also twice your age and otherwise taken."

"Duh. Like I'd do anything about it, anyway. Even if he wasn't," I add.

"Maybe he'll have a hot assistant helping him out."

Assistant? Is she kidding? Um, yeah, no one would be hotter than Nick Knight. He's legit steaming. Wow, I can't even imagine having a man like that as a boyfriend. The hotness would overwhelm me.

I know I said before that I wanted a man and not a boy. But, looking at Nick...he's so much man that I'd have no idea what to even do with him. *Whatever.* It doesn't matter, I tell myself. He's off-limits.

When I meet him, I will shake his hand and smile politely. I will model my ass off and show him that I am a force to reckon with; an up and comer that he needs to keep his eye on.

He will be thoroughly impressed with my professionalism and hard work. And, maybe, if I'm lucky, we will get to work together again at some point in the future.

If not, I'll tell him that it was a pleasure, board the plane and return home.

Back to my lonely, little apartment here at Sunset Terrace.

Chapter Four: Nick

As the plane levels off and begins the quick trip from LAX to Las Vegas' McCarran Airport, I sit back in my seat and decide to research the new model I'm going to shoot. *What the hell is her name? Sienna? No. Sierra? No.*

Savannah. Yeah, that's it.

All these Millennial names sound the same, I think, as I type Savannah Hart into the search engine and a bunch of pictures pop up. I click on one and study her. She's young and gorgeous with long, blonde hair and bright blue eyes, but it's more than that. She knows how to work the camera to show off her best angles and features.

I tilt my head and scroll through more pictures. *Damn.* She's got that certain, intangible quality that's going to make her a star. I can recognize it a mile away. *And, I'm going to launch her career,* I think.

Hmm, my mind goes into creative mode and I start imagining the different shots I'm going to take. That face of hers is everything I love to work with-- so malleable. In some of these pictures, she looks like a sexy temptress while in others she looks like an innocent virgin.

For the Guess shoot this weekend, we are going to the Neon Boneyard where defunct signs from old casinos and other businesses go to die. Iconic signage from the Stardust, Riviera and The Sands sit outside, baking in the sun, and we get to play with it all. A million ideas begin to bounce around in my head about how I can shoot this beauty in such a glamorously tragic setting.

I zoom in on her expressive blue eyes. There's no discernable expression on her face in the picture I'm looking at, yet her eyes convey a story. It's not some stupid, half-squint that Tyra Banks calls "smizing." It's a deep emotion that connects the viewer to her. The girl drips with raw talent and I can't wait to pull it all out of her. Push her to get the most amazing shots of her career. And, hell, probably even mine.

I feel better knowing that I have some promising talent to work with and pull up a personal story that some Ohio paper featured on her. Probably her hometown, I think, and scan down the article. *"My real dream is to become a vet in a few years. I plan to save the money I make modeling and use that to put myself through school and open up my own practice."*

Interesting, I think. Sounds like she may have half a brain in her head. Or, that's just the story her publicist made up for her. Nowadays, who the hell really knows? It's all about creating an image for the public to consume and adore. Now, with social media, the goal is to get millions of followers.

I do not have any type of social media account and I never will. It's a complete waste of time.

All I care about is following my rules. And, when I'm working with a gorgeous model, my most important rule is professionalism and absolutely no fraternizing with the talent. As a photographer, I've never crossed that line. The sleazy stories of a photographer coming on to a model are all too familiar.

I am no one's stereotype. Not anymore.

Back when I modeled, it was probably even worse than today. Everyone hooked up with everyone. I'm not going to pretend I was innocent and didn't take part in the shenanigans because I did. But, I've done some growing up since then and have had my share of enough beautiful women to realize something.

They're all the same. Purely ornamental. Worthless baubles. A swimming pool with no water.

That may sound harsh, but it's been my experience. So, the fact that I see a spark of life in this girl's eyes makes me stand up and take notice. For the first time in a long time, I'm excited to shoot a model. My normally jaded outlook evaporates and I scroll through one amazing shot after another of her.

When we land in Las Vegas 45 minutes later, I step off the plane and roll my carry-on behind me. We're booked at The Cosmopolitan and it's a quick drive to the chic hotel over on The Strip. Las Vegas is an interesting place to visit, but after a few days, I'm usually ready to get the hell out of here. However, I don't feel any rush on this trip. I plan to work hard and enjoy it. And, if things go well, maybe I'll take Deirdre up on her offer and spend an extra day lounging by the pool.

As I check into the 5-star luxury hotel, it's nice to not be the one footing the bill. My smoking credit card can stay in my wallet for once. I get my key and find the elevator bank to the tower that leads to my room thirty floors up.

I like the modern and sleek feel of the hotel and my room is no exception. It's stylish and whimsical which is exactly how I'm planning this photoshoot to be. I let go of the handle on my luggage, walk over and slide the balcony door open. I have a view of The Bellagio's fountains and it's stunning.

I glance down at my watch and it's already 4pm so I dig my phone out of my pocket and call my agent. "Hey, Deirdre, it's Nick. I'm here."

"How was the flight? Is the room okay?"

"All good."

"Okay, perfect. I emailed you the call sheet and Sienna will meet you at the restaurant tonight at 6pm for a little meet and greet."

"Savannah," I correct her.

"Oh, right. If you have any questions just give me a call."

"Sure thing, Deirdre. Thanks."

We say goodbye and I disconnect the call. I have two hours until I have to go down and meet Savannah so I grab my notebook, a pen and sit out on the balcony. I prop my long legs on a table, cross my ankles and start jotting down all of the ideas I have for tomorrow's first day at the Neon Boneyard.

Next door, The Bellagio's fountain show begins and I pause as music fills the air and water gushes into the sky. I've always enjoyed it and I'm glad my room faces this direction. A crowd gathers around and I decide to get out of my room and wander around until I have to meet Savannah.

On my way out, I grab my camera. My favorite thing about Vegas is the people-watching. You get every kind here and the photo ops are always there. I probably look like a tourist as I wander around the hotel and snap pictures. The colors, the textures and the inventive details of the decor are inspiring and I get so many cool shots.

I love the floor-to-ceiling chandeliers over the bars and move around the area getting some interesting pictures. The time flies and, before I realize it, I have about half an hour until our meeting. I decide to head over early and get a drink at the bar. The reservation is at Beauty & Essex and I'm not sure what to expect when I walk through the faux pawn shop storefront.

But, inside, it doesn't disappoint. The place has an upscale speakeasy vibe to it and I sit down at the bar and order a Jack on the rocks.

And then I wait. I hope Savannah has a personality to match her talent. So many of the models I've worked with just rely on their looks and trying to have a conversation with them is like pulling teeth.

I have zero expectations. To be honest, I just need to showcase that innate talent she possesses and get the job done. If she isn't a witty conversationalist, which I'm guessing she's not, it's fine.

After all, it's just two days of work.

It's not like I'm planning to spend the rest of my life with her.

Chapter Five: Savannah

After I land at the airport, I catch a taxi at the curb. "The Cosmopolitan, please," I tell the driver.

I can't believe I'm here. It's only about two miles to the hotel and the moment we hit Las Vegas Boulevard, my eyes go wide. "Oh, wow," I whisper and press my nose to the window. I have never seen anything quite like it.

"First time in Vegas?" the driver asks with a knowing smile.

"Yes," I say, unable to look away from the towering hotels and endless tourists walking down The Strip. There really are no words to describe the vibrancy and life pulsating through the city. When we pull up to the hotel, I slide out and wait as the driver lugs my suitcase out of the trunk.

"Don't get into too much trouble," he says with a wink.

"Oh, I won't. I'm here for work." I smile and thank him then start toward the front doors. There are probably 100 people checking in and plenty of counters to do it. I walk up and it doesn't take long to get my key and head toward the elevator.

Thirty floors up, I step off, find my room and unlock the door.

"Holy crap," I say and wheel my suitcase inside. It's freaking amazing with a huge bed, enormous bathroom and a giant TV up on the wall. My eyes are practically popping out of my head as I slide the balcony door open and step out. I lean over the rail and look down at a huge pool with fountains soaring straight up into the air. Lights blink and it's like the water moves with the music.

"So cool," I whisper.

I've never seen anything like Las Vegas, I think, and look out over the stunning view. I didn't really have any expectations coming here, but I'm kind of blown away. Earlier, I spoke with my agent and she said I'm supposed to meet Nick Knight at some place called Beauty & Essex at 6pm.

It's already after 5pm, I realize, and head over to my suitcase. I want to freshen up and look good, not like I just stepped off an airplane. I fix my makeup, curl my hair and change into one of the cute outfits that Jazz put together for me.

Thank God for Jazz, I think. I didn't even think about dressing up or having a meeting tonight. I can't even imagine meeting my photographer at some fancy restaurant in leggings and that plaid shirt I almost brought.

Good Lord, I would've looked like a complete country bumpkin, straight off the farm.

Instead, I slip on a cute swing dress and sandals. The hotel is a little chilly so I grab my little sweater, purse and phone.

And, I'm off.

I'm feeling a little overwhelmed when I walk into Beauty & Essex. There are crystals hanging from the ceiling and large velvet settees everywhere. I feel completely out of my element. It's still early and not very crowded. But, even if the place was packed, I couldn't miss the handsome man sitting at the bar.

Nick Knight.

My stomach gives a little flutter and I bite the inside of my lip. *You can do this.* I push my shoulders back and head over to where he waits. He's taking a sip of his drink when I move up beside him. "Nick?" I ask.

Silvery-gray eyes flick my way and he swallows the whiskey down hard. When he starts to choke, my eyes go wide. "Are you okay?" I ask.

He nods and clears his throat. "Fine," he manages and sets the glass on the bar. "You must be-"

"Savannah," I say and extend my hand. He reaches out and grips my hand, looking at me with this strange, almost bemused, expression on his face. God, he's just too good-looking and that makes me nervous. And, when I'm nervous, I talk.

A lot.

"It's so nice to meet you," I gush and continue to shake his hand. "I'm really looking forward to working together. I've heard so many things about you and I have a feeling we're going to have a really great time this weekend."

When his dark brows shoot straight up, I realize that may have come out wrong. Oh, God, the last thing I want is for him to think I'm being unprofessional. I'm talking too much and this is turning awkward, but I can't seem to stop my mouth. "On the shoot, I mean. I've never booked a campaign this big, but don't worry because I plan to work very hard. I think it's going to be a great experience for both of us and I look forward to getting to know you better and working with you and-"

"Savannah," he says, interrupting me. He looks down and I realize that I'm still pumping his hand like an idiot. I let go and wipe my palms on my dress. "Relax."

I nod, but suddenly, I wish I could walk back out the door and re-do this entire introduction.

"Our table is ready," he says in a low voice and stands up.

I'm tall at 5'11" and rarely meet guys who are my height or taller. But, Nick is a good five inches taller and I have to look up at his face. And, I really like that. As we follow a server over to a corner table, I sneak a peek at his chiseled profile. He's even better looking in person and I'm not surprised he used to model. It would've been a shame if he hadn't shared all this glorious hotness with the world.

Nick pulls the chair out for me and I sit down. Then, he moves around the table and sits, eyes glued to me. I'm not sure what it is, but something in his intense, dark silver gaze makes me flush. I grab the folded napkin and lay it over my lap, not sure what to say.

"How was your flight?" he asks.

"Fine. How was yours?"

His mouth edges up. "Good, thanks. What would you like to drink?"

As if on cue, the waiter appears. "Another Jack on the rocks?" he asks Nick.

"Sure," Nick says.

"And, for you, miss?"

"Um..." I grab the menu and open it. I don't normally drink so that's a good question. My brow furrows as I scan down the unfamiliar, fancy alcoholic beverages. I literally have no idea what I might like. Finally, I look up. "Can I just get some water?" I ask in a small voice. Yeah, I feel like the country cousin, straight off the plane from Hicksville.

The waiter nods "Sparkling or flat?"

"What?" For a second, I'm not sure what he's asking, but then I realize. "Flat," I say quickly and glance at Nick who's looking at me with a completely blank expression. God, he probably thinks I'm the most unsophisticated person he's ever met.

After the waiter walks away, Nick leans his forearms against the table and laces his fingers. "So, Savannah, what made you decide to become a model?"

"Well, I was always told I have the body for it," I say and instantly regret my choice of words when his gaze drops. "I mean because I'm skinny. Or, I used to be. I guess I've filled out since then." I give my head a shake realizing this meeting is not turning out the way I had hoped. I can't help it. Nick is too gorgeous and it's making me nervous as hell. And, all I wanted to do was impress him.

I look down and start picking at my nail polish. I wish I could crawl under the table.

"Any other reason?"

He sounds bored. "Um, well, the money is good."

The waiter returns and sets our drinks in front of us.

"Inspiring," he says and lifts the whiskey up to his lips.

His comment irks me and, after I sip my water, I meet his challenging gray gaze head-on. "It's not my dream," I clarify. "I'm modeling because-"

"Because it comes easy to you?"

My eyes narrow. What's he inferring? That I have no talent and I'm just some dumb blonde with an empty head? "No. Because it's a quicker path to what I really want to do with my life."

He lifts his glass and swirls the amber liquid around. "And, what's that?" he asks, sounding completely uninterested.

Suddenly, Nick Knight isn't as attractive as I thought earlier. I don't care for his nonchalant, arrogant attitude. Just because I'm younger than him doesn't mean I'm some insipid little girl. "I'm going to be a veterinarian," I announce proudly.

"Because you love animals so much?"

"That's right."

He raises that annoying brow again and I get the urge to flick it with my finger. "But, you wear leather shoes."

"What?" His comment catches me completely off-guard.

"Your sandals. They're leather, right?"

What a jerk, I think. But, he had me. For a moment, I don't say anything. But, that doesn't stop him from digging the knife a little deeper.

"I just figured a big animal lover would be a vegan. Or, at least, someone who avoids wearing animal carcasses." He smirks and takes another sip of his drink.

Is he trying to get under my skin? I wonder. What did I do to make him be so incredibly rude? I'm so annoyed, I can't even think of a comeback. Instead, I flip my menu open and focus on the different choices. Underneath the table, my knee is bouncing and all that nervousness from earlier morphs into aggravation.

And, dislike.

I decide that I do not like Nick Knight and the rumors about him being a pain in the ass to work with are obviously true. The whole thing puts a damper on my mood. So much for an amazing weekend in Vegas with a talented photographer.

Then, it hits me. He has the power to make my pictures look like shit if he wants. He literally holds my career in his hands. *Ugh.* The thought makes my stomach hurt.

When the waiter returns, I look up at him with a smile. "Do you have a vegan menu by any chance?"

Nick lifts a hand to cover his mouth and, for a second, it almost looks like he's smiling behind it.

"Of course," he says and returns with one a moment later.

I look over the unfamiliar food and inwardly groan. *Yuck, yuck and yuck.* I end up deciding on some pea-crusted tofu and hope it's edible. Meanwhile, Nick orders the New York Strip steak with a sly smile in my direction.

I look away, checking out the other customers and cool decor. Neither of us says anything and the coolness grows until it's like frost hangs in the air between us. *God.* We definitely got off on the wrong foot and I feel like I need to do something to fix that.

But, I didn't do anything. He's the one who started being rude. *It's my career, though,* I remind myself. Just suck it up and do a little ass-kissing. "So, Nick..." I say. "What made you decide to become a photographer?"

"I enjoy taking pictures."

"And, that was always your dream?"

"No," he admits. "I started out as a model, but got bored fast. As you know, it's not exactly challenging work."

What a dick. I feel my eyes start to narrow, but I stop myself from getting angry and focus on remaining positive.

"One day, I picked up a camera and decided it was better being on the other side of the lens."

"Are you from L.A.?"

"I live in Los Angeles, yes."

"Me, too. What part?"

"Malibu."

Of course. With the rest of the rich snobs. But, I can't help my curiosity. "On the beach?" I ask a little wistfully, feeling a tinge of envy. I always dreamed of living on the beach one day.

He nods, clasped hands below his chin, studying me closely.

"That must be nice," I say, completely sincere. "Falling asleep and waking up to the sound of the ocean."

He clears his throat. "I like it."

"When you open your back door, do you step right out onto the sand?"

Again, he nods.

My mouth curves up as I imagine living in a house like that. It's probably $10 million or more. "I'm jealous," I say and pick up my fork, twisting it around. He's looking at me again in that very intense way of his, this time at my mouth, and it's making me nervous. I hit the fork against my plate and it dings loudly so I quickly lay it back on the table. "What's the best part?"

His gaze lifts from my mouth to my eyes. "Sorry?"

"About living on the beach?"

His gray gaze penetrates mine. "The beauty. It's like, sometimes, you can't look away. It sucks you in, captivates you. Take my breath away."

My stomach flips at his words and his low, intimate tone makes me wonder if he's still talking about the beach. I get the feeling this conversation just went somewhere else completely.

Chapter Six: Nick

Savannah Hart is doing all those things to me and more. I'm literally having a hard time looking at anything else. Just find myself moving my gaze from her full lips up to her bright, aqua eyes and then sliding back down to those goddamn tempting lips again. She's wearing some kind of shiny gloss on them and-

This isn't good. Rules, Nick. Remember, your rules. Savannah Hart is the reason you have them in the first place.

I have always prided myself on my self-control. Especially when it comes to work. But, something about this girl is making me a little crazy. She gives off this artless, innocent vibe that heats my blood and is so completely different than the experienced women I've known.

It's important to keep my distance so, right away, I have to be a little bit of a dick. I feel bad about the leather shoe comment, but I don't want her to think we're friends. And, I certainly don't want her looking at me with those big, blue eyes like she did when she first walked up to me at the bar.

When I nearly choked to death, I think, remembering how she looked at me like she had a crush on me. She took me completely off-guard. I didn't expect her to be so beautiful. And, I don't just mean the physical. Her pictures may be flawless and amazing, but, in person, Savannah has this glow, an aura, that is so refreshing and it pulls you into her orbit. Like gravity.

And, I can't have that.

Just keep her at arm's length, Knight. Not that hard. It's only two more days.

When our dinner arrives, the timing is perfect. I shouldn't have made that last comment because it wasn't about the damn beach at all. It was about this mesmerizing girl sitting across from me.

I decide I need to shut up for a while and just eat. As I dig into the expensive steak, I notice Savannah begin to pick at the tofu, not looking overly thrilled. Amused, I chew and watch to see what she's going to do.

When she looks up and catches me watching her, she stabs a big piece and pops it into her defiant, little mouth. A second later, her blue eyes widen in surprise and she starts coughing. Hard. She lifts the napkin and, I'm guessing, spits the food into it.

Tears fill those pretty eyes of hers as she grabs her water and takes a few gulps.

"Something wrong?" I ask even though I know the Japanese horseradish just burned the shit out of her mouth.

"It's so hot," she gasps.

"That would be the wasabi," I say in a dry voice. But, inside, I'm dying. Trying not to laugh. *Poor thing.* I'll bet she doesn't even know what wasabi is and had no clue when she ordered it.

"Oh," she mumbles. "I guess I missed that."

"I'd share my steak, but you being a vegan and all…"

"Right," she says and eyeballs my plate. "I wouldn't touch that animal carcass with a ten-foot pole."

Yeah, sure. "Why don't you order something else?" I suggest.

A frown creases her brow. "But, that would be wasting food."

"And?"

"And, I was taught you eat whatever you order. There are people starving in this world, you know," she adds in a prim voice.

When the waiter returns and asks how our meals are, I take pity on her. I don't know why. Maybe because I get the feeling she's hungry. Probably because she's watching me eat like she is one of those starving people in the world. "Actually, I'd like to order a side dish. Can you bring us some roasted cauliflower?" When she sits up straighter, I suppress a smile. "And, an order of the BBQ fries?"

Her eyes practically sparkle when I mention the fries.

"Of course."

While we wait for the sides, I decide we should probably talk about the shoot, the whole reason we're having this dinner together in the first place. "Have you ever been to the Neon Boneyard?" I ask.

"No. I've never even been to Vegas."

I nod and take a sip of my whiskey. "It's a pretty cool place. Great location for a fashion shoot."

"It's where all the big, old hotel signs are, right?"

"That's right. We'll have complete access to the place and I want it all to have a whimsical feel. You saw the clothes already?"

She nods. "My fitting was yesterday."

"Good. It's for next year's spring catalog so everything is light, flowy, ethereal." As the last word leaves my mouth, I realize instead of whimsical, it would be even better to go angelic. Make her look like an angel on high. If I capture the early morning light just right and behind her, I'll be able to emphasize her innocent look and make it appear that she's glowing.

This new idea starts getting me excited and I study her features. Those bright blue eyes and blonde hair definitely make one think of angels. She has some spice, though, too, and in some of the pictures, I could bring that out.

Fallen angel.

When the thought hits me, I know where I'm taking this campaign. Luckily Guess didn't give me any specific guidelines because, let's face it, I'm just that good. They're smart enough to let me take creative control and not try to box me into one of their boring, corporate, politically-correct concepts.

I tap the edge of my glass, caught up in my vision, and she squirms under my scrutiny.

"What?" she asks, now sounding shy.

"Just thinking about some different shots for tomorrow. Inspiration hit and now I can't seem to stop it." The way she can go from angelic to devilish, from innocent to sassy, makes me think of even more ideas.

Angel and Devil.

"Like what?"

"A play on good and evil. You have the ability to look sweet and innocent one minute and turn saucy and hot the next. If we use that tomorrow, we're going to get some brilliant shots."

"Oh. That sounds fun, actually."

"You sound surprised," I comment.

"I just wasn't sure what kind of ideas you had," she says.

The waiter returns and sets the side dishes on the table. "Help yourself," I say when she hesitates. That's all the invitation she needs and her fork plows right into the BBQ fries. Just like I knew it would.

"How old are you, anyway?" I ask out of the blue.

Between bites of the fries, she takes a sip of water. "I just turned 21."

Which makes me 21 years older than her. God, I suddenly feel old. Luckily, I have good genes and have been able to age gracefully so far. I work out five days a week and eat healthy for the most part. But, I do enjoy alcohol and even a good cigar occasionally. My hair is still dark and thick. Though, I have noticed a few silver strands at my temples lately. No doubt thanks to Margo.

For the most part, I feel like I did at 21. Physically, anyway. Mentally, however, I'm wiser and more jaded.

"How old are you?" she asks.

Why does she care? I wonder. "Forty-two."

She studies me for a moment and then bites into another fry. "You don't look 42."

My lip twitches. "And, what does a 21-year old think a 42-year old should look like?"

She shrugs. "More gray hair? A dad-bod?"

I chuckle. "I work hard to avoid both of those."

A smile lights her face and she drags the cauliflower over after demolishing the fries. She picks through it for a minute then pierces a floret. For someone who claimed to be vegan earlier, she barely looks like she could tolerate being a vegetarian.

"You don't like cauliflower?" I lean forward and stab my fork into a piece.

"No, I do. I'm just not sure about this other stuff," she says and pushes the gremolata to the edge of the bowl.

I pop the floret into my mouth and smirk. "The garnish?"

"There's an awful lot of it to just be garnish and, after my mistake with that wasabi, I'm a little suspicious."

Artless, I think. *Such a breath of fresh air.* "It's just parsley, a little garlic and lemon juice." When she raises a brow, I take another piece with my fork. "I promise."

"I usually pour Cheez-Whiz over my cauliflower. Or, melt some Velveeta on it."

I make a face. "Do you know what's in that crap?"

"Not wasabi, that's for sure."

I chuckle. "You're really something else. You know that?"

"Maybe it's an Ohio thing. Because it's really hard finding Cheez-Whiz out here."

"That's because it's disgusting."

"Shut up! It's delicious. Sometimes I just eat it right out of the jar with a spoon."

I pretend to shiver. "Let me guess. I bet you like that cheese in a can, too."

"Easy Cheese? Oh, my gosh, yes. I squirt that straight into my mouth."

The laughter dies in my throat when an image of her putting something wide and thick between those luscious lips and savoring it makes my lower body tighten. *Shit.* I let the conversation get too personal, steering away from business. And, I can't afford to do that.

I reach for my glass and toss the rest of the Jack Daniels back in one swallow. It's time to return to being a detached, cool professional. Although, inside I feel a low fire burning hotly. Just looking at Savannah stokes the flames. *Fuck.* I need to throw some water on it.

Nip it in the bud right fucking now, Nick.

This shoot is going to be a pain in my ass, I realize. Because I have a feeling that Savannah Hart is going to drive me crazy. Push me over the edge, if I let her.

But, I won't let that happen. I'm going to suck it up, be a jerk in order to not fan the flames and follow every one of my goddamn rules. Then, I'll go back home to my lonely life at the beach.

That's my plan, anyway.

It's funny, though, how sometimes fate steps in and creates an entirely new plan.

Certainly, one that I never saw coming.

Chapter Seven: Savannah

After dinner, Nick and I walk back up to our adjacent rooms on the thirtieth floor. Somewhere toward the end of dinner, he turned cool again and I'm not sure why. We started having a good conversation and just when I think he might be nice, after all, he shuts down.

Nick Knight is a moody artist, no doubt about it.

It doesn't matter, though. We're only working together for two days and I can totally handle anything he throws at me. If he wants to keep his distance and not joke around or get personal, that's fine by me. I have enough friends and do not need another one. Especially someone who runs hot and cold. People like that are the worst because you always have to tiptoe around them and never know what to expect.

As I pull out my key, Nick opens his door. "See you at 7," he mumbles.

"See you," I say and watch him disappear into his room without so much as a good night or nice meeting you. *What a grump.*

My call time is actually at 5am and I don't have the luxury of strolling in two hours later. Right now, though, I plan to soak in the huge bathtub until my skin wrinkles. I pull the La Perla nightgown out of my suitcase and head into the enormous bathroom.

While the tub fills, I pull my hair up into a messy bun and brush my teeth. Then, I wander over and dump some scented bubble bath under the faucet. I've never stayed in a hotel this fancy and I figure I may as well enjoy the amenities.

Once it's full to the brim, I slip into the steaming water and lay my head back. *Ohhh, amaze-balls.* The hot water smells like sugared-flowers and it helps ease the tension from my meeting with Nick.

Nick Knight. I wish I could stop thinking about him, but I can't. Since the moment Jazz showed me his picture, he's infiltrated my head. He isn't even very nice or cool, yet I can't seem to forget his silver-gray eyes and the way he just stared at me tonight.

What was he thinking? I wonder. Did he regret taking this job after meeting me? Maybe he thinks I'm a flake or ditzy since I couldn't stop babbling after introducing myself. He's just so incredibly handsome, older and talented. I felt completely out of my league the second I walked into the restaurant and met him.

Get it together, I tell myself. You can't act like some teenage girl swooning over a boy band singer. The moment Nick got snarky, though, I stopped seeing him as this perfect man and for the jerk he was inside.

I suppose as long as he stays cool and aloof, everything will be okay. I won't fall to pieces every time he lays those metallic eyes on me.

Little do I know…

After my bath, I dry off and slip the La Perla nightgown over my head. It's soft, silky and completely luxurious. I spritz some of my favorite perfume, Vera Wang's Princess Night, on and feel just like royalty.

In a sweet cloud of velvety jasmine, vanilla and sugar, I head over to the balcony to check out the nighttime view of Las Vegas. And, it doesn't disappoint. Lights blink everywhere and this is definitely a city that doesn't sleep. Crowds of people walk down the boulevard and suddenly the dancing fountain down below at The Bellagio comes to life and music pours through the speakers.

As I lean out over the railing and watch the show, I realize someone else is doing the same thing one balcony over. My heart gives a little stutter and I pull back and out of sight the moment I realize it's Nick.

"Enjoying the show?" his deep voice asks.

I move closer to the divider that separates our balconies. I can't see him, but his powerful presence is palpable. "Every time it starts, I come out to watch," I admit. "I've never seen anything like it before."

For a moment he doesn't say anything. Then, "Yeah, I know what you mean."

I move closer to the privacy wall between us, feeling bolder. He can't see me and for some reason it's so much easier to talk to him like this now then it was earlier at the restaurant. "I'm looking forward to working with you. I think your work is brilliant."

I hear him walk over to the divider, maybe lean a shoulder against it. "Thanks. I, ah, think you're pretty talented yourself."

"Really?"

"Yeah."

I feel a huge smile stretch across my face. "Coming from you, that means a lot."

As the show below ends, I lean my head against the wall between us and gaze out at the city.

"Goodnight, Savannah," he says.

"Goodnight, Nick." I wait for him to move back into his room, but don't hear anything. A few minutes later, a cool breeze blows over me and my skin breaks out in goosebumps reminding me of the tiny nightgown I'm wearing. I rub the chill from my arms, turn and go back into my room.

As I slide the glass door shut, I finally hear Nick do the same.

The next morning, it takes me ten minutes to Uber down to the Neon Museum. The massive outdoor exhibit has more than 200 signs on display that once adorned the casinos and hotels of vintage Las Vegas. It's like a giant picture book of Vegas history and I'm pumped that we get to shoot here.

There are a couple of big pop-up canopies set up out back and, the moment I appear, the hair and makeup team usher me under one. I feel like Katniss in The Hunger Games as they go to work, primping and polishing, pulling out all of the stops to get me camera-ready.

By the time Nick steps on set two hours later, I'm ready. The team did a phenomenal job and I can't wait to get in front of the camera. He walks over, takes one look at me and frowns. "No. This isn't what I want," he says. "She's supposed to look like an angel not a hooker."

My mouth drops open and the team descends. "She's wearing way too much makeup," he complains. "And, why is her hair so big? Make it straight and sleek. Why am I doing your job? Jesus."

Without even a greeting to me, or to anyone else for that matter, he launches into one complaint after another. "I'm sorry," I whisper to Leah, the girl trying to fix my makeup. "I thought you did a great job."

"Thanks, sweetie. Just close your eyes. I'm going to lighten your eye shadow up."

For a moment, Nick stands there and glares. *We get it, you're unhappy, Geez. Go away.* But, he hovers around, keeping a close eye on their work. "Get rid of all that blush. She should look pale, almost translucent." He shakes his head, curses and stalks away to check out the set.

"Is he always this pleasant?" I ask and they all stifle giggles.

"He's an artist," Leah says. "They can be temperamental."

"That's no excuse to be rude," I say.

I notice the team exchange amused looks and I'm willing to bet they feel the same way, but are too scared to say anything. Nick Knight is the type to steamroll all over someone if they don't speak up and I really wanted this to be a pleasant experience. Now, I'm getting worried.

Maybe he will chill out after a coffee, I think, and watch him accept a styrofoam cup from an assistant. He's conferring with the crew and directing the setup of various lights around a huge sign that says Stardust.

Twenty minutes later, the team finishes re-doing my look and calls Nick over to get his approval. He stands just outside the awning and motions for me to stand up. I slide off the stool and he crooks a finger at me. "Come here," he says. "I want to see you in the natural light."

I move out into the early morning sunshine and he studies me closely with a critical eye. God, I feel like I'm under a microscope beneath those narrow, gray slits. "Fine," he says. "Get her dressed before we waste more time. We're already losing the early light I wanted."

"Maybe you should've come earlier," I mumble.

"*What?*" The sound is like a low hiss and I stop in my tracks.

Oh, crap. I honestly didn't think he'd hear me. I glance over my shoulder and try to play it off. "What?"

"Is there a problem, Miss Hart?"

"No. All good."

"Then get your ass in there and get dressed," he orders between gritted teeth.

I don't bother to respond, just hightail it into the tent where the wardrobe waits. I slip out of the robe and they pull a pretty white sundress over my head. It's long and flowy and laces up the front which also makes it sexy. They place a huge hat on my head, some chunky jewelry, sandals and then push me out.

No one follows and I look over my shoulder to see them hover at the tent's entrance, watching, waiting for Nick to criticize their work. He takes one look at me and says, "Lose the hat."

I pull the floppy thing off my head and Leah takes it.

"Over there," Nick says and points to the letter "S" on the sign. Again, he narrows his eyes, studying me. "Take the jewelry and shoes off, too."

I do as he says, then wait. He moves closer, camera in his hand. "Lounge against it."

It's time to lose myself and let my instincts take over. I lean into the huge letter, pull the long skirt up to reveal my lower legs and try to convey the angelic look he mentioned last night. He snaps a couple times then shakes his head.

"No. Give me more than that."

I change my position up and his frown only deepens. I try a few other angles, play with the dress and alter my expressions, but nothing seems to make him happy.

"Move to the other letter."

"Which one?" I ask.

With an annoyed sigh, he lifts a finger and points to the "A."

When I move to the new letter and begin to pose, I've never seen anyone look so irritated. He crosses his arms and raises a dark brow. "What're you doing?" he asks in a clipped tone.

I have no idea what I'm doing wrong and the nerves I've been trying to suppress hit me hard. Everyone is watching-- the lighting guys, assistant, hair, wardrobe and makeup teams. I feel like an absolute idiot.

"Um-"

"The "R." I pointed to the "R" so why you're standing at the "A," I have no idea. Put your listening ears on, Sienna."

Utter humiliation washes through me and I move over to the opposite letter. The next 30 minutes goes on like this with Nick giving unclear directions and me trying to understand what he wants. Trying to please a man who obviously can't be pleased.

He doesn't utter one word of praise. Just a string of orders like some military commander. Most of the time he looks frustrated and completely vexed. And, it's starting to irk me the way he keeps calling me by the wrong name. I'm not sure if he's doing it on purpose or if he really forgot my name.

Either way, I bite my lip and do my absolute best to figure out what he wants and remain quiet, just absorbing his jabs and maintaining a completely professional attitude. Jazz told me Nick is the one who's such a professional, yet I'm seeing everything to the contrary.

He's being a first-class asshole and I have no idea why. I guess for whatever reason, he just doesn't like me. Well, that's fine because I don't like him, either.

"Sienna! Pay attention. I told you-"

"Savannah," I correct him. Let him be mad. *Whatever.*

For a moment he doesn't say anything. But, the how-dare-you look on his face makes me instantly regret opening my mouth.

"Oh, excuse me," he says, voice dripping in sarcasm. He stalks closer until he's within a foot of me and I can see I'm about to get reamed. "You know why I can't remember your name? Because you're nobody." He lets that sink in then continues. "In order to make it, to have people recognize you and actually remember your name, you need to work hard and prove yourself. And, so far, I've seen very little of that today."

My eyes slip shut and I feel my cheeks heat up and turn red. *Jerk.* I can't believe this. I've been working my ass off all morning and don't deserve the disrespect he's showing me. But, I bite my lip and take it. Nick has the power to fire me and if that happens, I will be truly humiliated.

"I suggest you stop dicking around and start modeling," Nick adds. "Otherwise, I'll be forced to find someone else who can actually do the job and who has the brains to understand what I'm asking. Is that clear, Sienna?"

I bite my cheek so hard it bleeds. *I hate this pompous prick.* Seriously hate him with a passion. "Crystal clear, Mr. Knight," I say in as pleasant a voice as I can muster and give him a saccharine smile.

Chapter Eight: Nick

As I click the camera, I wonder if I went too far. I'm being an asshole. I know I am, but what's the alternative? Compliment her and tell her how great she's doing? No, I want her to get better. Not be complacent.

I'm going to challenge Savannah Hart until she reaches a new level of perfection. And, yes, maybe I'm being more harsh than necessary, but it's also important that she keeps her distance. If she hates me then she won't come around and tempt me with those big, blue eyes.

"Head up," I snap. When she lifts her golden head and looks up to the sky, a ray of sunshine hits her just right. And, something hits me in the gut. It's low and fierce. *Desire,* I realize, and try to push it away.

Rule number three, Knight, I remind myself.

But, God, she's stunning. She literally looks like an angel. Or, after all my berating, maybe the better term is martyr. So young, so innocent. I give my head a shake. What the fuck is wrong with me? I'm supposed to be working and all I can think about is if she tastes as sweet as she looks.

And, that damn perfume. I don't know what it is, but the moment I smelled it yesterday, I wanted to lick her. It fits her-- some combination of sweet and a faint dash of spice. Last night when she came out onto the balcony, it wafted over and teased me to the point that I wanted to hop over that divider and devour her.

Instead, I lingered out there and let the scent envelop me. Then, I went back inside and jerked off.

She's getting under my skin and the only way I know how to cope is to lash out. I'm being unprofessional, a complete ogre. But, what choice do I have? I have to keep my distance and that's all there is to it.

Our relationship is strictly a professional one and that's how it's going to remain.

We move over to a new sign and, while the crew sets up, I watch her move off to the side and sigh. I can tell that she's frustrated, but Savannah is a trooper. No matter what I throw at her, she lobs it right back. She's knocking this whole photo shoot out of the park, but I'll be damned before I tell her that.

The moment I laid eyes on her last night at the restaurant, she shook me. Hell, I choked on my drink. I'm not sure what I was expecting. Probably just another ditzy, empty-headed model, but the young woman I met was so much more than that. She possesses such a sweet, wide-eyed innocence and the nervous way she stumbled over her words and shook my hand for a minute straight was endearing.

And, frustrating. I don't want to feel the overwhelming attraction that's stoking a heat inside me. But, it's there and doesn't seem to be going away no matter what I do.

Fuck.

Without her realizing it, I snap a picture of her standing there, the wind blowing the gauzy dress up, the blazing blue sky and mountains behind her. *I'm keeping this one for me.* When the crew is done setting up, I motion for Savannah. We're working with the old Moulin Rouge sign and the letters were rearranged at some point to spell out "In Love." I give her some clipped direction and she follows it perfectly. *Of course, she does,* I think and struggle not to roll my eyes.

If this were any other girl, I'd be thrilled. Despite the grief I'm giving her, she's listening and taking direction like a seasoned pro. We shoot for a while longer and then it's time to break for lunch. But, I'm not hungry and I wander off to take a break far away from everyone else. I'd like to be out of earshot when they start talking shit about me.

I find a bench in the shade and start scrolling through the hundreds of pictures I've taken so far today. Normally, when I'm going through shots, a good one will pop up every 20-30 pictures or so, but literally every single shot of Savannah is exquisite. The client is going to be thrilled and have a really hard time choosing which photos to use.

Savannah Hart is on the verge of catapulting into super stardom.

I'm glad to be the photographer who captured these flawless shots. I like the feeling that I'm the one responsible for bringing this kind of magnificence out of her. But, deep down, I know she had it in her way before she met me.

And, after this shoot? Photographers are going to be banging her door down to work with her and I'll just be some faded memory. Maybe an anecdote in a future magazine article about the worst experience she ever had on set.

My eyes narrow. Well, the day's not over yet so I can still give her some good material for that article.

All of a sudden, I look up and see a mangy-looking dog nearby. The poor thing looks half-starved and is probably dehydrated from this desert heat. I stand up and head over to the craft service tent where I load a plate up with some lunchmeat and cheese. I grab a bottled water and make my way back out and over to where the dog lays curled up beneath the shade of a large sign.

"Hey, pup," I say and approach the dog slowly. "You hungry? Want some chow?" I drop down and sit cross-legged on the ground. The dog perks up and eyes the plate of food. I whistle, encouraging him to come over. "Don't be scared." After a few more low, encouraging words, the dog gets up and makes its way over. I hand him a piece of ham and he takes it with utmost gentleness. "That's a good boy." Poor thing must be a stray. I've heard that people will drop unwanted animals off in the desert and it makes me sick. At least have the decency to take him to the pound where he has a chance to find a new home and be safe from coyotes and other prey.

For the next 20 minutes, I feed the dog and talk to him quietly. I think he's probably the only one on set who likes me. It doesn't take long before he's sprawled out next to me, offering his belly and I give it a good rub.

He's a scruffy-looking thing and absolutely filthy. I wonder how long he's been wandering around out here, all alone, lost and hungry. *Dammit.* The last thing I need is a dog, but I'm already trying to figure out how I can get him home. I'm not leaving him out here to die, that's for sure.

I glance down at my watch and realize it's time to get back to work. The dog helped turn my mood around and I decide I'm keeping him. I scratch his head then stand up. "Don't go anywhere, buddy. You just hit the jackpot."

I motion for my assistant to come over. "Noah, I need you to help me out."

"That's why I'm here. Whatever you need, Nick"

"Find something I can use to leash this guy up. Then, I want you to drive him to the nearest groomer and get him the works. Bath, trim, nail cutting." Noah frowns. Probably not what he expected, but whatever. "Make sure the place can board him overnight."

"Okay." He's looking at me strangely, but I don't care.

"You're from L.A., right?" When the kid nods, I say, "Great. If I pay you a few hundred bucks, will you drive him back and drop him off at my house?"

"Sure." Noah looks pretty happy now that he knows he doesn't have to deal with me for the rest of the weekend.

"Thanks. Text me your info and I'll Quickpay you."

"Yeah, cool, thanks, Nick."

"Appreciate your help on set, Noah, but now you're in charge of this guy."

"Does he have a name?"

I look down at the dog who is maybe some kind of shepherd mix and then nod. "Yeah. Paul."

"Sounds good and don't worry about a thing. I'll make sure he's all cleaned up and then bring him to you in L.A."

I nod, give Paul another scratch behind his ear and say, "See you soon, buddy."

As Noah handles the dog, I wander back to set and head over to the next place I want to shoot. It's a huge shoe with a sign behind it that says Silver Slipper. When the others see I'm ready, they all jump up and get back to work. We take some time to set up the lighting and then Savannah appears in a short robe.

And, my heart slams against my ribs.

Shit, I totally forgot we had to shoot her in a bathing suit. I try not to pay attention when she slips the robe off and steps on set, but it's impossible. Everything in me stands to attention and I curse under my breath.

The too-tiny, metallic bikini shimmers in the sun and starts a wildfire within me. Her curves are slim and elegant. Those long legs seem to go on forever and her perfect breasts are high and perky and, if I had to guess, a full B-cup.

I grit my jaw so hard, I'm probably on the verge of breaking a tooth. *Relax. Just fucking breathe, Knight.* I suck in a deep breath and motion to the slipper. *Yeah, great direction.* But, I'm scared if I try to speak, my voice will come out raspy and disjointed. Or, worse, crack.

I swallow hard and then do the only thing I can. What I've been doing all day. I turn into a complete dick.

"Up on the shoe, Sienna. Let's go, we haven't got all day. Jesus."

She doesn't say anything, just climbs up.

"Lean back. Stretch out on it." She does it, but looks far from relaxed. I'm not sure whether it's because of me or the minimal clothing she wears. "Relax. You look like an uptight virgin."

Something flashes in her aqua eyes and, for the first time, I wonder if she is a virgin. The majority of models I've met are fast and loose. *Holy hell.* Could it be true? The fire inside hits a new intensity and I need to quench it fast.

"Fucking, relax, I said. It's not that hard."

"Sorry," she murmurs.

"Don't be sorry, just listen. Now, arch your back. Straighten that left leg out…"

She does everything I say, but I'm not getting the shot I want. All I'm getting is the beginning of a hard-on. And, it's pissing me off.

"Sienna! Bend your leg. Jesus."

"You said to straighten it!"

Did I? Fuck if I remember. This little girl has me so mixed up right now, I don't know right from left or up from down.

"Bend it, goddammit," I hiss. Then, I stalk right up to her and lean down into her face. I lower my voice so only she can hear me. "And, if you ever correct me again, I'll throw your scrawny ass off my set."

Frustrated tears fill her eyes and, before I even realize it, she slides off the huge shoe and shoves past me, snatching up her robe. I watch her run away and I shove a hand through my hair. Guess I finally pushed her too far.

And, I feel bad.

Shit.

Everyone looks awkward and no one says a thing. I throw the camera strap over my shoulder and stalk after her. I end up finding her on the bench I sat on earlier and drop down beside her. I know I went too far and need to apologize. But, she's driving me crazy. I've never been so attracted to anyone like this.

"Sorry," I mumble. "You didn't deserve that."

She swipes at her nose and when she looks over at me, I've never seen eyes so incredibly blue. Like the Caribbean Sea.

"I was so excited for this shoot, but...I don't think I want to work with you anymore," she says.

This should've been one of the best experiences of her life and I ruined it. I turned into a verbally-abusive asshole because I didn't like the way she was making me feel. *Not cool, Nick. So not cool.*

"Savannah-"

"Don't you mean Sienna?"

I let out a sigh. "I'm an asshole, okay?"

"No, it's not okay," she says and frowns. "And, if that's your attempt at an apology, it really sucks."

I feel the corner of my mouth edge up and have to give her credit. She's a saucy little thing when she wants to be. I look up at the lowering sun and know it's time to call it a day. I got every shot I wanted plus 1,000 more. "I sincerely apologize. Truce?"

For a moment, it doesn't look like she's going to forgive me. She's really taking her sweet time, actually, and I arch a brow. Finally, she relents. "Truce."

The softly-spoken word fills me with an odd sense of relief. "Let me make it up to you and buy you dinner. Since neither of us ate lunch."

She gives me a strange look, surprised that I knew she didn't eat, too. But, of course, I knew. I spent every other second of the break, surreptitiously watching her while I was petting Paul.

"You don't have to," she says.

"I insist." When she gives a slight nod, I stand up. "I'm going to let the crew go."

"We're done?"

"I got all the shots I wanted and then some." I start to walk away then turn back. "You did great today," I add in a low voice.

A surprised, half-smile curves her mouth. "Thanks."

"I'll come over at 7 to get you for dinner."

"Okay."

A few minutes before 7pm, I pace back and forth in my room. I've showered, shaved and changed my shirt twice. I feel like I'm about to jump out of my skin. I don't know what my problem is, but I've been acting nuts all day. Since the moment Savannah stepped on set and nearly made me forget to breathe.

That's what it is about her. When I'm in her presence, I forget. I forget to be professional, forget to be polite, forget my rules, practically forget my own goddamn name. All I can focus on is her. I want tomorrow to be better on set than today's fiasco so it's important I smooth things over at dinner.

I just hope Savannah Hart is a forgiving person and we can maintain our truce.

Just one more day, I tell myself. Then, we go our separate ways. At exactly 7pm, I walk over and knock. As the door swings inward, my mouth drops open a fraction. Savannah wears some slinky red dress and heels that make her look even more tall and slender than usual. She reminds me of a long-stemmed, red rose and I feel a stirring below my belt.

I try not to read too much into it. She's a model. She's beautiful. *Aren't they all?*

"Hi," she says and steps out into the hallway. "Where are we eating?"

"Um, I made reservations for Top of the World."

Her eyes light up. "Where's that?"

"It's at the top of The Stratosphere. The dining room revolves 360 degrees every 80 minutes."

"Oh, my gosh, how fun."

I figured she might like something quintessential Las Vegas. Especially since it's her first trip here. A half an hour later, we're sitting at a table beside the large window, looking out over the blinking lights of the city. Actually, I'm looking at Savannah and she's gazing out the window. The view out the glass may be nice, but the view across the table is even more spectacular.

"This is amazing," she says. "You can see the whole city."

"Wait til it starts to spin."

"Ooh, I can't wait," she exclaims.

I open my menu and see a few vegetarian choices, but nothing vegan. "Are you really a vegan?" I ask.

She gives me a sheepish look. "No. I tried to go vegetarian once, but then I realized I couldn't eat my Mom's chicken and dumplings and, well, there's no way I can give those up."

"I kind of figured by the way you kept eyeballing my steak last night."

"I did not," she says. "Well, maybe a little."

"You're not originally from L.A., are you?"

"Nope. How'd you guess?"

"You're normal."

She laughs. "I'm from Ohio and I think I know one person who's actually a native Californian. She lives in my apartment complex and, I can assure you, she's quite normal and very nice."

When the waiter comes over, I order my usual Jack Daniel's and she orders water. "You don't drink?" I ask.

"Not really. I guess every blue moon."

"There's a blue moon tonight," I say and scan down the drink menu. "You like salty or sweet?"

"Sweet," she says, eyes sparkling.

"Can you make the lady a Kir Royale?" I ask.

"Of course."

After the waiter walks away, she leans forward. "What's that?"

"It's a French cocktail made with Creme de cassis which is a berry-flavored liqueur and champagne."

"That sounds delicious."

"It's about as sweet as you can get."

"I don't know a lot about alcohol so thank you for ordering for me."

"You're welcome."

I feel like I should apologize again for today, but I don't want to even bring it up. Things are going smoothly right now so I decide to wait until after we've both had a couple of drinks.

"So, you still have family in Ohio?"

She nods. "My parents and younger sister live there. I miss them, but it's nice to be out here, chasing the dream, you know?"

"When this campaign launches, I think you'll have achieved your dream."

"I hope so. Like I told you, I'm saving money for school."

"To be a vet."

She nods and the waiter returns with our drinks.

I watch closely as she lifts the glass and takes a sip.

"Well?"

"Oh, my gosh, delicious! Where has this drink been all my life?"

I laugh. "Didn't you just turn 21?"

"Yes," she says with a perfect smile. "Last month." For a moment she doesn't say anything, but then she frowns. "I kind of regret not having a party. My neighbors wanted to throw me one, but I said no."

"You didn't go out on your 21st birthday?"

She shakes her head. "I'm not a big party girl."

"So, you rarely drink, you don't like to party...What do you do?"

"I work a lot and I like to, ah, read."

I can't help it. I just blurt out the question that's been like an itch in my mind all day. "And, spend time with your boyfriend?"

"I don't have a boyfriend."

Wow. This beauty is far too gorgeous and smart to be staying inside and reading. *What a waste,* I think. Maybe there's something I can do about it, though.

"Okay, now you're depressing me," I say. "I think it's time you let loose and have a little fun. For Chrissake, you're in Vegas. The city requires you to do something wild and outrageous."

"Otherwise, I'd be doing a disservice to the city?" she asks with a saucy smile.

"Exactly. You'd be giving Sin City the finger and I don't think I can let that happen."

"So, what do you propose? A drunken night out on the town?"

"Sure. Among other things."

Our gazes meet and there's a brief flare of heat in the depths of her bright blue eyes, but then she looks away. "My friend pretty much said the same thing before I left. That I should celebrate a little."

"Your friend sounds very wise."

"I guess I've just always been the good girl," she admits and finishes her drink in one, long swallow.

God, a dark, dirty part of me would love to change that.

Dinner and dessert are delicious and, by the time it's over, we've each had three drinks. I'm fine, but I can tell Savannah is tipsy as hell. After paying the bill, we head out to the elevator and right when I'm about to hit the down button, she grabs my hand. "Wait," she says, aqua eyes glowing.

With mischief? I wonder and look down at her slim fingers wrapped around mine.

"I'm not ready to go back to the hotel yet."

I raise a brow and feel her squeeze my hand.

"Wanna play?"

The invitation makes my cock turn rock-hard. "Play what?" I ask, voice suddenly husky.

"How about Truth or Dare?"

I frown, not quite sure where she's going with this. But, what I do know is the more I find out about her, the more I like her. The attraction is dangerous, but I can't help it. She mesmerizes me on every level. Especially when she said she's always been a good girl.

Christ. I'm willing to bet my last dollar that she's a virgin. That's never been a turn-on for me before, but now I can't stop thinking about it. "Yeah, okay," I say. "I'll play."

A smile lights up her face and she claps her hands.

Maybe I shouldn't have let her drink three Kir Royales. *Oh, hell, who cares?* She's earned it.

"Truth or Dare?" she asks me.

"Dare," I say.

She points to the sign on the wall that advertises SkyJump. "I dare you to do it."

"Are you joking?"

"Are you scared?"

I narrow my eyes, knowing she's got me right where she wants me. *Vixen.* "No, I'll do it."

Instead of down, I hit up and we head to the roof and, all the way, I think I must be losing my damn mind. Yet, 20 minutes later, I'm strapped into a harness, standing at the edge of the roof and on the verge of leaping off. I'm glad I had those three drinks.

I look over at Savannah and she's positively glowing.

"I think you should jump, too," I say.

"I think I'd rather meet you at the bottom," she says with a wink.

"You're really something," I tell her. Then, heart pounding, I turn and step off the building, 829 feet above the street. And, fuck me, it's exhilarating as I plummet down at over 40 miles an hour. I zoom down to the landing pad while the crowd below gasps and applauds.

What a rush. My heart's still in my throat as they help me take the harness off. As I walk over to the hotel's entrance to meet Savannah, my legs feel like rubber. I could easily throw the dare back in her face because I know that's what she's going to pick. But, I have other plans.

When she flies out the front door, she's laughing and full of life. "I can't believe you actually did that! You're braver than me."

I do kind of feel like a superhero and, still riding on the high, I grab her hand and lead her around the corner. "Your turn," I say. "Truth or Dare?"

And, just like I knew she would, Savannah chooses dare. And, I'm ready. "I dare you to let me kiss you." Her eyes flash blue lightning and I move closer, pushing her back against the wall. When I lower my face to hers, I feel her arms snake around my neck and then I brush my lips against hers.

I place my palms above her, flat on the cool brick and, other than my lips, I don't let myself touch her. I hold back, not wanting to scare her and doing my best to keep the kiss on the innocent side. Well, as much as I can. I just want her to relax and let go. I don't let myself think about the possible repercussions. I only enjoy her soft lips and how she tastes like berries.

It's okay, I tell myself. *We're just playing a silly game. It doesn't mean anything.*

Chapter Nine: Savannah

When Nick lifts his head, I have trouble catching my breath. *Oh, wow.* Even though his kiss was that of a complete gentleman, I felt it all the way down to my toes. I don't have much experience kissing guys and I've certainly never kissed a man as old as Nick.

But, something about him being a little older makes me feel safe, protected and like I can trust him. I hope I'm not fooling myself.

All of my life, I have always played it safe. A boring, predictable good girl. Well, not tonight, I vow. Tonight, I'm going to have some fun. And, maybe a couple more of those absolutely fabulous Kir Royales.

I slip out under Nick's arms, still propped up on the wall and sashay away. When I don't hear him immediately follow, I glance back over my shoulder to see him leaning against the wall, arms now crossed. I think he's checking out my ass, but I can't be sure. "Are you coming?" He gives me a funny look then walks over.

"Where to now?" he asks.

"I want to do all sorts of things tonight. Things I've never done before."

"Okay. And, I'm supposed to be the bad influence who encourages you?"

"Something like that," I say with a little smile.

"So, give me the list. What haven't you done?"

I think for a moment. *Pretty much everything worth doing,* I realize. "Well, I've never danced at a big, fancy nightclub or gambled in a casino or sipped cocktails at a piano bar or walked around on the arm of an extremely gorgeous man."

Nick slants me a look then places my arm in the crook of his. Leaning into him, I can feel the warmth of his skin through his shirt and the hard muscles that flex in his bicep. I see how other women look at him, like he's a dessert they want to gobble up, so I feel special walking beside him like this.

Nick is the most gorgeous man I have ever met. And, now that he's finally being nice and even flirty, I'm having all kinds of devilish thoughts. The alcohol I consumed makes me not dwell on his earlier behavior during the photo shoot and allows me to sweep it under the rug. For now, anyway.

I still can't believe he kissed me. God, I feel like dancing. "Truth or dare?" I ask him.

"If I pick dare, are you going to make me jump off another hotel?" he teases.

"No," I say and laugh.

As we make our way back up The Strip, Nick looks down at me and whispers, "Dare, then."

"I dare you to dance with me at the hottest club in Vegas."

"I don't dance," he says.

I tilt my head and look up at him. "Are you declining my dare?"

"No, just warning you to have low expectations when it comes to my dancing skills."

"I'll assume you have other skills to make up for your poor dancing?" I ask in a teasing tone.

I hear him draw in a breath and then he leans down, lips so near that I can feel his warm breath tickle my ear. "I do. Skills that a nice girl like you would know nothing about."

My stomach somersaults at the insinuation. As I try to get my rapid heartbeat under control, Nick pulls out his phone and pulls up a search. I look down to see him type in "hottest nightclub in Vegas," and I can't help but laugh.

"You're as big a dork as I am."

"Baby, I'm 42. I haven't been to a club in 20 years."

We end up at the MGM Grand where apparently the place to be is Hakkasan. The cover charge is outrageous and I almost change my mind, but Nick pays and tells me it's Vegas. It's huge and sprawls over 80,000 square feet with five levels of dance floors, lounges and restaurants. We go up to the third-floor where there's 10,000 square feet of dance floor and a couple of lounges.

The main room pumps EDM/house music and a DJ spins in an upper balcony. The dance floor is surrounded by numerous VIP tables arranged in a semicircle facing the DJ booth, giving every table a great view. Giant LED screens flash images with the music and an intense light show makes the entire room look surreal.

I feel like I'm in a dream as I grab Nick's hand and pull him into the huge crowd of dancers. All of my inhibitions are gone thanks to the three drinks at dinner and I lift my arms above my head and let the music take hold. I've never felt so completely free and I sway my hips to the beat, lost in the rhythm.

At this moment, I don't think about the past or the future. I just enjoy the present and fully commit. Then, I realize Nick isn't dancing. He's just standing there and watching me, the flashing lights highlighting his sharp cheekbones.

I reach out my hands and, after a brief hesitation, he laces his warm fingers through mine. I draw him forward until I can smell the citrusy snap of his aftershave. *God, he smells good.* I pull my hands out of his and run them up his hard chest.

His hands drop to my hips and I can't stop touching him. His pecs, his upper arms, the back of his neck...I let my fingers drag over his toned upper body and love the feel of it. He's so very masculine and my senses are going wild.

I can tell he's holding back, though. Almost like he's scared to touch me back. *And, that is simply unacceptable.* I close the distance between our bodies, my lower body brushing against his, and I can't miss his swift intake of breath.

"Savannah..." he says, his breath warm against my ear again. Shivers race up and down my spine.

I can hear the warning in his tone, but tonight I'm going to play with fire. I'm going to play with Nick Knight. "Just dance with me, Nick," I tell him and push closer.

The moment he lets his guard down, I know. He spins me around, yanks me back against him and there's no mistaking the hardness that presses into the curve of my lower back. I freeze up for a second then push my ass against him. What can I say? The alcohol I don't normally drink is making me do things I would never do sober.

His long fingers dig into my hips as we find a rhythm and move together to the pulsating beat of the music. When I drop my head back against his shoulder, I feel him press a kiss to my neck then drag his mouth up to my ear. He doesn't say anything, though. Just keeps his warm lips near my ear and I love the feel of his hot breath rustling my hair.

And, suddenly, it occurs to me that I could have sex with Nick Knight tonight.

Oh, no. From somewhere deep down, a voice of reason pushes through the alcohol haze. That probably isn't the best decision. As hot as he is, we still have to work together tomorrow. And, I hardly want him to find out that I've never had sex before. God, I'd die of embarrassment.

But, it's not like I'm saving my virginity for any specific reason. I'm not waiting for marriage and I'm not overly religious. I lead such a busy life that dating and sex have just been relegated to the back burner. But, now, I wonder if I'm missing out.

I'm wondering if I should spend the night with Nick.

Oh, my gosh, the thought makes me break out in goosebumps. And, with my luck, probably hives. Suddenly, I feel hot and overwhelmed. Too many people surround us and I can't breathe as the light show starts again. It's making me feel dizzy and when someone bumps into me, I'm ready to get away from the hot, sweaty crowd. "Can we go?" I ask Nick.

A frown furrows his brow then he takes my hand in his and leads me off the packed dance floor. "Sorry," I say. "I just need some air."

"C'mon, this way," he says and leads me toward an exit.

When the cool night air hits me, I breathe deeply and instantly feel better. Also, more sober.

"You okay?" he asks, concern in his voice.

I nod. "There were just too many people."

"One of the reasons you tend to stop going to nightclubs after you hit 23," he says with a smirk. "I have a much better place we can go and it'll be something you can cross off your list."

Nick again tucks my arm in his and we wind up at a piano bar at The Bellagio. It's an upscale, elegant lounge and jazz music fills the dark, cozy air. He guides me out onto the patio and we sit at a table that overlooks the fountains with the Paris Hotel and its huge replica of the Eiffel tower in the background.

It's so stunning and romantic.

Nick orders a Jack Daniels from the server and lifts a dark brow. "Another Kir Royale or are you all set for the night?"

"Yes, please," I tell the waiter. "And, I'm not even close to being all set for the night," I say to Nick.

When his mouth edges up, I don't think I've ever seen a more attractive man. It's getting late and I notice the dark stubble coming in on his angular jaw and it makes my lower belly curl with heat. I have no idea what he's thinking or feeling, but I decide to just enjoy this once-in-a-lifetime night with him.

I don't want to think about tomorrow. Just admire those silver-gray eyes that are focused so intently on me.

"So, Savannah," he says. "Truth or Dare?"

My heart catches and I smile. "Truth."

"Really? Okay, let me think for a sec."

"I just have a feeling that if I pick dare you're going to have me jumping into the fountains," I say.

He chuckles. "Actually, that's a good one." His gaze rakes over my face as he decides what to ask. "But, I wouldn't want you to ruin that dress. It looks beautiful on you, by the way."

A flush warms my face and I smile. "Thank you." Just in time, the waiter returns with our drinks. Nick continues to study me over the rim of his glass as I sip my new favorite alcoholic beverage. *Delish.* I fish a raspberry out and pop it into my mouth.

I notice Nick's nostrils flare and he downs half his drink in one long swallow. "Well? What's your question?" I ask.

He sets the glass down, index finger running back and forth over the edge. "I'm trying to come up with a more appropriate one because all I seem to have are extremely inappropriate questions running through my head."

My heart begins to thump madly and I bite my lip. "According to the rules of the game, you can ask whatever you want."

Something feral, almost possessive, flashes in his eyes. "How many men have you slept with?" he asks in a low voice.

I swallow hard and take another sip of my drink. He's either going to really like my answer or be done with me. I meet his gaze and tell him the truth. "None."

"Are you waiting for someone?"

I debate how to answer and then decide to stick with the truth. "I think I've been waiting for you."

"Fuck, Savannah," he growls. He reaches out and drags my chair closer until my knees bump his hard thigh. "Don't say things like that."

"Why not?"

"Because you're making me so hard it hurts."

"Oh, I didn't realize…"

"Of course, you didn't," he says.

Beneath the table, I feel his hand move over my knee then slide beneath the hem of my skirt and touch my bare skin. It's electric and I draw in a raspy breath. He trails his warm hand up and down the inside of my thigh and a very wicked part of me wants him to go higher. But, he doesn't.

A muscle flexes in his jaw and he sips his drink. "You are every man's fantasy," he says.

I feel warmth radiate through my whole body at his words. "You're not too hard on the eyes, either," I tell him and he laughs.

"What am I going to do with you?" he asks.

"What would you like to do with me?" I ask, feeling bold.

He releases a low breath and leans closer. "You don't wanna know."

"Actually, I do."

Nick lifts my chin, gaze locked on mine, and kisses me again. But, this time it's different. Not so sweet. It's hotter and more demanding. His mouth opens and I follow his lead. When his tongue slips between my lips, I shyly meet it with mine and he groans before pulling away.

Then, his phone rings. He reaches into his pocket and checks the caller id. An annoyed look crosses his face and he silences the call and flips the phone over on the table. "Sorry. It could've been about the shoot tomorrow. Now, where were we?" He leans in and, just as he begins to kiss me again, his phone starts vibrating.

Nick pulls back and smothers a sigh of aggravation. "Will you excuse me? If I don't answer this, she won't stop calling."

She. Oh, my God. I wonder if it's the girlfriend that I completely and conveniently forgot all about. Here I am thinking about sleeping with someone else's boyfriend and then his significant other calls. Suddenly, I feel like the biggest asshole.

"Hello?" he answers and sits back in his chair. "Now's not the time. Because I'm in Vegas...working."

I'd hardly say he's working right now, but whatever.

"Yes, a photo shoot," he says and runs a hand through his hair. "I don't have an answer for you."

I can hear a feminine voice on the other end of the line and she doesn't sound happy.

"Look, I have to go. I already told you-"

Nick holds the phone away from his ear, looks at me and mouths "sorry." I force a half-smile, but I don't feel very well all of a sudden. My stomach hurts and I can't believe I've been running around Vegas acting like I don't have a care in the world. Kissing a man who is now on the phone with his girlfriend.

I know they say what happens in Vegas stays in Vegas, but I'm not down with that. I tried, but that's just not me. I scoot my chair back, cross my legs and pull my dress down.

"Margo, I'll talk to you later, okay?" He hangs up the phone and studies me. "Sorry about that."

"Your girlfriend?" *Yeah, buddy, you're busted.*

For a moment he doesn't say anything. Then, he grabs his glass and finishes his drink. "Actually, we broke up."

I blink, not sure what to say or think. "Oh."

"How did you know I had a girlfriend?"

"Um, you're gorgeous. And, I did my research before the shoot," I admit. He nods, not looking happy about the conversation or the call. "Why did you break up? If you don't mind me asking."

"Because I don't love her," he answers without hesitation.

"That's a good reason." When his mouth edges up in that adorable smile that makes my insides quiver, I feel better. Knowing they aren't together anymore is a relief because I'm really into this man. Like I've never been into anyone before.

I'm so curious about him and I want to know everything there is to know about Nick Knight.

"Have you loved a lot of women?" I ask and finish my drink. The question can be taken a couple of different ways and I'm wondering how he will choose to answer.

"Are you asking me how many women I've loved or bedded?"

I shrug. "Either. Both." Even though I'm dying to know how many people he's been with, his number is probably so high that it'll make me nauseous.

"It's not my style to carve a notch on my bedpost after every fuck, but I'm not going to lie. I've had my fair share."

When he doesn't say anything else, I press further. "And, love?"

He scoffs. "Love isn't for me."

"What do you mean?"

"I don't fall in love, Savannah. It makes you vulnerable and miserable when things eventually don't work out. Because, trust me, they never do."

"Well, that's depressing."

"So is having a romanticized view of the world. Life isn't a fairytale and if more people realized that, they'd be better off."

"It sounds like someone got his heart broken and now he's jaded."

"No. I never got my heart broken because I already told you-- I don't fall in love."

I listen to his words, but I always believed that loving someone just happens. It's not something you have control over. I guess Nick just hasn't found anyone yet who has been able to stir up any kind of deep emotion within him.

I rest my chin in my hands and study the emotionally-crippled man before me. I don't care what he says, something happened to him to make him have such a negative attitude about love. "Poor Margo," I say.

"It is what it is. She wanted things I couldn't give her." Nick flags the waiter and orders us another round.

"I don't know if I can drink anymore," I say. "But, I'll try," I add and he chuckles. "Now, I believe it's my turn, so...Truth or Dare, Nick?"

"I'm probably going to regret this, but truth."

Good. Exactly what I was hoping he'd say. I'm about to put it all out there and either our night is just about to begin or end abruptly. Maybe I'm a glutton for punishment since Nick just told me he doesn't fall in love or have any kind of deep connection with women, but I don't care.

A part of me wants this man so badly, it makes me ache. I take a deep breath then spill it. "If I ask…will you spend the night with me tonight?"

Hunger flares in his eyes. "Yes," he says in a raspy voice.

My heart drops at the single word and a million butterflies beat their wings inside my stomach. "Good to know," I say.

His silver eyes narrow. "Wait a second. So, let me get this straight. You haven't actually asked me?"

"Nope."

He barks out a laugh, eyes crinkling at the corners. "Well, that's about the most half-ass invitation I've ever received."

When our drinks arrive, we down them. I think we both know that I *did* ask him and now all we want to do is return to the hotel. To one of our rooms. The second we finish, Nick is on his feet and pulling me up with him.

The patio spins and I grab onto his arm. "You okay?"

"Just a little drunk," I say and teeter to the side.

"I got you," he assures me and loops an arm around my waist.

As we make our way back to The Cosmopolitan, I feel my nerves kick in. Right before we head inside, I pretend I need some extra fresh air and we sit on a bench. I basically just asked Nick to be the first man I go to bed with and he accepted. My head is spinning and not because of the alcohol I drank.

I think I just went too far and I looked over at him.

"You okay?" he asks.

Am I okay? I'm honestly not sure until I look into his gray eyes and see exactly what I need-- assurance, strength, someone who wants to be with me. I'm not sure how else to really explain it. I just know what I feel in my gut-- that he wants me, I want him and this is our night to make that happen.

A blinking sign makes me look up and I see a wedding chapel across the way. Suddenly, the doors fly open and a couple walks out. They're absolutely glowing and all over each other. I chuckle then hear Nick's deep voice in my ear.

"Truth or Dare?" he asks. From the serious tone in his voice, I don't think he's playing games anymore.

Thirty minutes later, after I accepted Nick's dare, we are the ones stumbling out of the wedding chapel. I suppose I could blame it on all the alcohol and my low tolerance or this silly game we've been playing all night. Or, the idea that Nick is running from his ex or I'm just tired of being the lonely virgin who sits at home every night and works far too hard for someone so young. Hell, maybe we are both just two very lonely people.

Maybe it's a combination of all that.

But, when I said "I do" without an ounce of hesitation in that cheesy chapel, it was because when I looked into Nick's eyes, I saw the other half of me. The connection was kinetic and the pull unlike anything I've ever felt before.

I wanted this man in my bed and now, after a few words from an Elvis impersonator, he's my husband. *Oh, my freaking God,* I think.

Back at The Cosmopolitan, Nick opens the door to his room and when I move to walk inside, he holds up a hand. "Hang on," he says. "We have to do this properly, Mrs. Knight." Then, he sweeps me off my feet and over the threshold.

He kicks the door shut, walks over to the bed and sets me down. Then, he sits down next to me.

"Are we crazy?" I ask.

"Probably a little bit," he admits. "But, hey, it's Vegas. Go big or go home."

"That's right," I say and then cover my mouth after I hiccup.

He scrutinizes me closely. "How drunk are you, by the way?"

"I love how you ask me that after we're married."

"What?" he asks, all innocence. "You think I would've chanced you running out on me at the altar?"

I reach up and lay a hand against his stubbly face. "I'll never run out on you, Nick," I promise.

He blinks as though he's not quite sure he fully believes me, but he also doesn't want to think too hard about it.

"For someone who rarely drinks, you can hold your liquor pretty well, sweetheart," he says.

"I think saying 'I do' sobered me up pretty quickly. You?"

"I'm fine."

Now that we're here, back in the room and all alone, reality begins to set in and I give him a nudge with my elbow. "You, ah, know that you didn't have to marry me to sleep with me tonight, right?"

Nick chuckles then he reaches over and pulls me onto his lap. "What can I say? I love a good dare," he whispers and begins to kiss my neck.

His soft lips moving over the delicate skin makes my pulse spike and I tilt my head to give him better access.

"Are you nervous?" he asks and pulls back to meet my gaze.

I give a little nod. "Yes, but more excited than nervous."

"You have nothing to worry about, sweetheart. I'm going to take good care of you tonight."

"Will you be gentle with me?" I ask, a teasing note in my voice.

"I'm going to move so slowly and bring you so much pleasure, you're going to be coming all night."

A flush warms my cheeks and Nick stands up and begins unbuttoning his shirt. I watch, unable to look away, and when he shrugs it off, I get my first view of his perfect chest. *Oh, my.* It's smooth, hard and the six-pack lets me know he works out regularly.

When he crooks his finger at me, I stand up. "We better get that dress off before it gets ruined."

I turn and he slides the zipper down oh-so-slowly, his knuckles grazing my skin. I'm so glad Jazz made me pack some sexy underwear otherwise I'd probably have brought my plain, comfortable cotton ones. But, I'm wearing satin and lace, and as the dress falls off, I watch Nick's reaction.

A fire burns in his silver eyes. "God, you're beautiful." For a moment, he just lets his gaze roam over me and I suddenly feel self-conscious. When I lift my hands to cover myself, Nick's arm snakes out and he grabs my wrist. "Don't. Your body's too perfect to be covered."

Nick unbuckles his belt, slides it loose and then unbuttons his pants. He moves back over, gathers me in his arms and lays me on the bed. A moment later, he slides up my body and takes my mouth in a long, slow kiss that awakens every nerve-ending in my body.

God Almighty, this man knows how to kiss.

When his tongue slides against mine, I reach up and run my fingers through his dark hair. It's longer on top and trimmed short at the nape of his neck and I love the silky feel of it. Nick's mouth lowers, leaving a trail of kisses down my throat and then down further, licking along the tops of my breasts. He grasps the straps of my bra, pulling them down, and marking me with wet kisses. Then, he unsnaps it and tosses it aside.

His big hand curves over my breast, lifting it, molding it and when he pulls my taut nipple into his mouth, I let out a soft moan. "Do you like that?" he asks. I give a shy nod. "Then, you're going to love when I suck on your...on other things."

Heat floods through me and I have a feeling he's censoring his words. Trying not to shock me and I appreciate the thoughtfulness. I don't think I'm ready for dirty talk yet. I run my nails lightly down his back and his head moves lower, mouth gliding over my stomach, swirling around my navel. "I'm going to make you feel so good," he promises.

His fingers hook into the elastic of my panties and then they're sliding down my thighs and landing on the floor beside my bra. Completely naked now, I've never felt so vulnerable, so exposed. Nick moves back up and I try to relax, but the nervous virgin kicks in and I let out a shaky breath. "You okay, sweetheart?"

"Mm-hm," I say and squeeze my eyes shut, but he must feel me tense up.

"Look at me," he murmurs.

When I open my eyes, he's right there, brushing my hair back and luring me into the silvery depths of his gaze. "I love your eyes," I say, unable to look away. "They're all melty and metallic."

His mouth curves up. "And, I love everything about you." He drops a butterfly kiss at the corner of my eye. "Your bright blue eyes…your soft lips…" He captures my mouth in a kiss that leaves me breathless. "Your perfect breasts…" His mouth dips and he licks from one breast to the other. "Your stomach…" I suck in a breath as he licks down my flat stomach to a hip bone. "And, most of all, I love how you're all mine," he says and slides a hand between my legs, cupping me.

I suck in a sharp breath. But, when Nick's long fingers begin to stroke me, I lean back and let the sensations flow over me. Those smart fingers tease and swirl and apply just the right amount of pressure to make me twist and writhe. I start panting and feel my breath hitch when he slides a finger inside me.

"God, you're wet. And, so tight."

I'm guessing that's a good thing because I can hear what almost sounds like awe in Nick's suddenly hoarse voice. I forget all about my earlier nerves and instead focus on the increasing pressure that's making me tighten around his finger. All of a sudden, waves of pleasure start radiating throughout my lower body and I jerk when his mouth replaces his fingers.

"Nick-" I gasp and push up on my elbows. His tongue laps up my folds and then his lips wrap around the swollen bud above. "Oh, my God…" I pant hard, hear my raspy breathing, and try to clamp my legs together.

"Let go, Sav," he murmurs and pushes my legs further apart. "Don't fight it." When he pulls that most delicate, throbbing part of me into his mouth again and sucks, something inside me shatters. My body arches up and pleasure shoots through me, rippling out to touch every corner of my body.

My eyes roll back, I twist the sheets in my hands and I can't believe what I've been missing out on all this time.

Chapter Ten: Nick

As I move back up Savannah's body, leaving a trail of hot kisses, I can't believe how responsive she is and how fucking good she tastes. Just when I think I could get used to her delectable, little body, I remind myself she's mine. *All mine.*

Earlier, when we were sitting on the bench outside the wedding chapel, two things crossed my mind. One, that if I married Savannah then all of her belonged to me. All that wide-eyed innocence and all that tempting sexiness that she keeps simmering just below the surface. And, second, I'd be able to collect my inheritance and rid myself of Margo.

So, here I am. A married man and to hell with rule number three. I still plan to keep my emotions in check and dominate Sav in the bedroom so we're all good with the others.

Yeah, it was an impulsive decision, but I need that money my Grandmother left me. The sooner I tie the knot, the better. So, it may as well be with someone who's young, innocent and beautiful like Savannah. Unlike Margo, Sav is practically a baby and someone I can mold. Someone I can teach and enjoy without pushback. Someone who won't drive me into the poor house and an early grave.

I'm not sure what to expect, but I don't regret my decision and so far, so good. Granted, we've only been married an hour and I'm in the middle of fucking my new bride, but I have high hopes.

Sure, she's younger, but I don't care. And, the fact that she's so innocent and I'm the first and only man she's ever been with makes me feel possessive and protective. I came so close to proposing to Margo, a first-class bitch, and Savannah is the complete opposite. A breath of much-needed fresh air.

I kiss her, making her taste herself, and then draw back. I'm ready to rip through my zipper, but I promised her I'd take it slow. But, now that she's wet and throbbing, I get up and drop my pants and boxer briefs. She watches and I like the look that brightens her eyes. It's curiosity.

Back on the bed, I move up and kiss her again. She's getting comfortable with me, responding back with enthusiasm, and I'm so ready to slide into her. *Patience*, I tell myself.

"How're you feeling?"

"Good," she says and runs her tongue between her lips, looking down. "Should I, ah, do the same thing to you now?"

Her words make my cock hard as granite. "Not tonight, sweetheart. Even though I'd like that very much, I'm going to take care of you tonight."

"I just want to make you happy," she says.

"You're making me ecstatic. And, don't worry, I plan to teach you everything I know."

"I have a feeling you know quite a bit."

I smirk. "One thing at a time, little girl."

"You have all these nicknames for me," she says. "I need one for you."

When she runs a hand down my chest, lightly scraping her nails over a flat nipple, I feel a jolt straight down to my cock. *Jesus.* "Baby girl, you can call me whatever you want. Call me Daddy for all I care."

"Daddy? That's a little kinky, isn't it?"

Without warning, I yank her down and press my hot, hard length against the inside of her thigh. "I like a little kink sometimes," I whisper and lick up the side of her neck. She's driving me crazy, making me so hot, I'm not sure how much longer I can hold out. And, then, all bets are off when she slides that hand between us and tentatively brushes her fingers along my rigid cock.

I snatch her hand up and hold it against the pillow. "You do that and I'm going to explode," I warn her.

"You feel like hot velvet," she murmurs.

Fuck. I'm done. I reach over and grab the condom. I assume she's not on birth control and the last thing I want to do is get her pregnant.

With heavy-lidded blue eyes, she watches as I rip the package open and roll it on. Then, I move between her legs, pushing them further apart, and line myself up. All I want to do is plunge into her hard and fast, but I grit my teeth and hover at her wet entrance. "I'm going to go as slow as I can, but I need you to relax, okay?"

Her fingers flutter down my back and she nods, eyes so full of trust. Breathing hard, I begin to push inside her and she immediately tenses up. "Easy, Sav," I say and pull back out. I reach down and start to massage her clit then slide in again, this time further. Back out again. In.

I let her body adjust to me then thrust in all the way. Savannah jerks and gives a little cry, but she's a fucking trooper, my girl. I kiss her hard and thoroughly as I start moving, finding my rhythm and guiding her hips with me.

All the while, I don't let up with my fingers, trying to find out exactly how much pressure makes her breath hitch. Makes her writhe and causes that little mewling sound at the back of her throat that's so fucking sexy.

"C'mon, Sav," I say, voice raspy. "Get there."

When her orgasm hits, I thank God and I'm right on her heels. The pleasure building blows and I groan as a shudder runs through me. I think I see fucking stars. Panting hard, I drop down beside her, a possessive arm across her middle. She glances over at me and asks me what I've been asking her all night, "Are you okay?"

I let out a shaky laugh. "Yeah. Are you?"

"Yes, Daddy," she says in a naughty whisper.

Fuck me, I think, as the realization hits me that this little girl I married on a whim in Vegas is going to be a handful.

A delightful handful. Just as long as she remembers who's really in charge.

Our call time the next morning is a bit later, but when the alarm goes off at 7am, I have to drag my eyes open and shake the cobwebs from my head. So much has happened in the last 24 hours and I'm not sure what to make of it.

Beside me, Savannah stretches that beautiful, lithe body of hers and looks over at me with a shy smile.

"Morning," I say.

"Good morning," she says, sitting up and pulling the sheet around her.

"Your head okay after all those Kir Royales last night?"

"A little bit of a headache, but I'll take a couple aspirin. I'll work hard today at the shoot so don't even worry about that."

"I have no doubts."

"I'm going to go back to my room and take a shower. My call time is 8am."

"Mine's 10am." I slide out of bed, pull my boxer briefs on and walk Savannah to the door. She's wrapped up in my sheet and carrying her dress, undergarments, shoes and purse. "See you soon," I say and press a kiss to her forehead.

Halfway out the door, she turns back around. "Nick?"

I pull my gaze up from the way the sheet drapes her hips like some Greek Goddess and arch a brow.

"You don't regret last night, do you?"

"Hell, no," I say. Her mouth curves in a smile and then she heads over to her room.

And, I can't help but watch until she disappears inside. Back in my own room, without Savannah, it suddenly seems...lonely and too empty. She has such a sweet and vivacious presence and the moment it's no longer there, I can feel the difference.

I'm not sure I'll ever fully understand what made me marry someone I barely knew 24 hours, but when she just asked me if I had any regrets, I can honestly say I don't. It's been a whirlwind, but a very pleasurable one.

With a yawn and stretch, I hop in the shower and get ready to go take pictures of my new bride.

Chapter Eleven: Savannah

I shut my door and slump against it, mind whirling.

I got married last night. *Holy crap.* As I try to make sense of everything that happened between Nick and I, I pull my phone out of my purse and see there's a message. It's from Jazz and I hit play: *"Hey, girl, I'm just calling to make sure you aren't holed up in your room, all alone. Your butt better be downstairs in that slinky red dress having a drink. Love you, babe."*

Well, I definitely didn't spend last night alone, I think, and feel the tender ache between my legs. My insides melt when I think about how Nick took his time with me. He was so tender and gentle. I can't imagine any other man treating me like he did and I'm so glad I waited for him.

For my husband.

God. I'm still trying to wrap my head around it. How that silly game turned into something so much more. He leaned his head in and his voice came out so very low when he asked, "Truth or Dare?"

"Dare," I whispered.

"Marry me," he said.

Maybe I should be wondering if I made a huge mistake, but if I listen to my heart, the answer is no. And, maybe that's crazy. Maybe we're both crazy. But, if this is what crazy feels like, I'm all in.

It occurred to me as I was leaving that Nick might have regrets, but he said no. *Hell, no.* And, he seemed happy and in a good mood. The complete opposite of how he behaved yesterday during the shoot. It'll be interesting to see how he acts toward me today.

I know that he can't possibly love me. Not yet, anyway, but I'm hoping the more time we spend together, the more his feelings will grow. Already, I can feel myself falling for him. Falling hard.

I decide that I'm going to be the best wife and partner in the world. I'll take care of him, support him and maybe even learn how to cook. I still want to work another year or two, but maybe I won't have to and can start school now.

So many thoughts flood my mind as I step into the shower and I'm really looking forward to seeing what the future brings.

When I get to the set, the makeup and hair crews descend and, by the time Nick shows up a couple of hours later, I'm the complete opposite character I was yesterday. Instead of angelic, I'm a temptress. My makeup is dark and smoky, my outfits today are more sexy and my hair is that perfect mussed bedhead.

When Nick walks onto set, he takes one look at me and pauses. I hope he's happy with the look they created. After yesterday, everyone tenses up, preparing for him to glower and start barking what he wants changed. Instead, he walks over to me, gaze moving from my head to my feet. "She looks amazing, thank you," he says and I think I hear the crew let out a collective sigh of relief.

"Savannah, can we talk quick?" he asks.

I slide off the stool and follow him over to a corner where we have some privacy. "Hi," I whisper, fighting back the urge to stand up on my tiptoes and kiss him.

"Hi, sweetheart," he murmurs. He glances over my shoulder at everyone and then back to me. "Let's keep last night our secret for now, okay?"

"From the crew, you mean?"

"Right. It's really not their business and I want everyone to focus on the shoot, not ask us a bunch of personal questions."

"Sure. That makes sense."

"Good girl." His heated gaze moves over me again and his mouth edges up. "You look like sex on a stick, by the way."

I smile. "Good enough to eat?" I ask.

He groans low under his breath. "It's taking every ounce of my self-control to not pull you into my arms right now and kiss you senseless."

I feel a bunch of curious eyes on us and I bat my lashes on him. "Good."

Unlike yesterday, the second half of the photo shoot goes smoothly and Nick's attitude toward me has the crew exchanging looks. They don't understand how he did such a complete 180 degrees, going from pompous prick to pleased photographer.

Because today, I can do no wrong. He compliments me nonstop, encouraging me with positive words. After each shot, he's nodding and telling me how great I'm doing. And, he's slipping in a lot of endearments like "sweetheart," "gorgeous," and "baby."

I model even better than yesterday because I thrive under the positivity he's showering over me. Yesterday, I felt like a wilting plant stuck in the desert heat while today, it's like the rain has brought me back to life and I'm flourishing.

Everything goes so well that we finish early. The good mood on set is contagious and as we wrap up, several people slant sly smiles in my direction. "Whatever you did to smooth things over, thank you," Leah, the makeup girl, says. "Believe me when I say we all thank you from the bottom of our hearts."

I can't help but blush. Oh, my gosh, if she only knew.

Nick and I are the last ones on set and, after saying goodbye to the last person, we hop in an Uber and go back to the hotel. "What do you think?" he asks. "Should we spend another night in Vegas or head home after we eat?"

"I wouldn't mind getting back tonight," I say.

"Yeah, me neither. We have some things to figure out," he says. "I'd like you to move into the beach house with me."

I can honestly say that I never thought I'd be living on the beach in Malibu. "You mean you don't want to move into my tiny apartment in crowded Hollywood?"

He chuckles. "Nah. I think you'll like Malibu better."

"Me, too. I will miss my neighbors, though," I add.

"They can visit," he says and reaches for my hand. When he twines his fingers through mine, I think about tonight and once again being alone with Nick. But, this time, we will be in his bed. My stomach flips and I squeeze his hand.

This is all so new. I've never had a serious relationship or been in love and now I'm suddenly married to a man I hardly know. In the back of my head, I know I have to tell my parents, but I'm in no hurry. I have no idea how they'll take it and I'm still trying to figure the whole situation out myself. I know they're going to have a million and one questions so I want to make sure I know the answers before I break the news.

Back at The Cosmopolitan, I change into a little dress and sandals and we head down to Holstein's Shakes and Buns. It's casual and offers all kinds of delicious burgers and a wide selection of craft beers. My eyes widen when I see their signature Bam-Boozled, alcohol-infused milkshakes and I consider ordering one, but since I'll probably pass out from the sugar rush, I decide to skip it.

Nick orders a burger smothered in cheese, bacon and tomatoes and I get a Caesar salad which turns out to be huge. I steal a fry off his plate and swipe it through the ketchup. "What's your favorite food?" I ask and pop it in my mouth.

"Probably my Mom's homemade macaroni and cheese. It's the best thing ever."

"I'll have to get the recipe from her," I say.

Something flickers through his eyes before he asks me the same question. "My Mom's a good cook, too," I tell him. "And her chicken and dumplings are my favorite."

Nick swallows a sip of beer and eyes me. "How do you think your parents are going to react to us getting married?"

"Usually, as long as I'm happy, they're happy. What about yours?"

"I'm going to have to explain about Margo and then you. It'll be interesting, that's for sure."

"They're in California?"

He nods. "Simi Valley."

"Well, I look forward to meeting them. What should I know?"

Nick shrugs a wide shoulder and wipes his mouth with a napkin. "We're originally from New York and I moved my mom and stepdad out here a few years ago. No brothers or sisters. So, my mom's been pushing me to settle down and give her some grandkids."

"And, she assumes that's going to happen with Margo."

"Exactly."

I take a sip of water and know I'm going to be so nervous when I meet his mom. "I hope she's not disappointed," I say. "Were she and Margo close?"

"Margo and my mother?" He laughs. "Hardly."

I wait for him to tell me more.

"Margo likes the finer things in life and my parents are from Buffalo. Let's just say they didn't have a lot in common."

"But, do they approve of her?"

Another shrug. "I guess. I mean, I never really asked."

Well, at least they weren't best friends, I think. It makes me feel better and gives me hope that his parents will give me a fair chance. "You said stepdad. Your parents are divorced?"

"Yeah. They separated a long time ago."

"Do you still talk to your real dad?"

At the mention of his real father, Nick's face goes blank. "John Keller is the only real dad I ever had."

I'm not sure how to respond. Then, from over my shoulder, I hear a feminine voice say, "Nick?"

Nick glances up and blinks in surprise. "Avery! How are you?"

A stunning blonde walks up to the table with a very tall, extremely muscular man by her side. Her cornflower blue eyes are bright and she's very, very pregnant. "Ready to pop," she announces.

"Congratulations," Nick says and stands up to give her a quick hug. "You must be Ryker," he says and extends a hand.

They shake and I can't help but notice Ryker's dark, rugged good looks. He also looks a little dangerous. Definitely someone you wouldn't want to mess with because he'd kick your ass with minimal effort.

"Ryker, this is Nick Knight, photographer extraordinaire. Nick, this is my husband." When she says "my husband," love fills her eyes and Ryker wraps an arm around her waist.

"Nice to meet you," Ryker says. "Ave told me you helped her out on a shoot a few months ago."

Nick nods. "That's right. Although, I think she was doing absolutely fine without me."

"I normally do weddings, not magazine covers," she explains. "I was really nervous so Easton set me up with Nick to get some pointers."

Avery glances at me and smiles. "Hi, I'm Savannah," I say, a little annoyed that Nick didn't introduce me yet.

"I'm Avery," she says and shakes my hand. "And, this is Ryker. And, this little girl," she says and points to her stomach, "is kicking up a storm."

When Ryker drops a kiss on her temple, she leans into his embrace. "I think Luka's about ready to come out," he says.

"I'm ready for that, too," she says and everyone chuckles.

I've never seen a couple look so happy and completely head over heels in love. They can't keep their hands off each other and Nick's pretending like I'm invisible.

"So, what're you doing in Vegas? Work or vacation?" Avery asks Nick.

"Work. We had a photo shoot for a new campaign." He nods at me.

Finally, he acknowledges me. Geez.

"Oh, that's exciting." She glances down at me. "I thought you looked like a model."

"Thanks," I say. I decide I really like Avery. She seems super sweet, genuine and looks so adorable in her little, pink swing dress. "I think *you* look like a model."

"Doesn't she?" Ryker agrees and tugs her closer.

Avery blushes and shakes her head. "Oh, no. I prefer to be on the other side of the camera, thank you very much."

"What about you?" Nick asks. "Vacation?"

"A little of both," Ryker says.

"Ryker works at Platinum Security and needed to meet a client here. So, we decided to make it a road trip. With the baby coming, this is probably our last chance. At least for a while, anyway."

"You must be so excited," I say.

They share a smile and the look in their eyes makes me a little jealous. Makes me wonder why Nick didn't tell them we were married. "Very," Avery says. "It's going to be an adjustment, for sure, but luckily little Luca has a lot of aunts and uncles at Platinum Security who are ready to help out and spoil her rotten."

"Griff and Jax just told me they ordered her a t-shirt that says, "My Daddy Is A SEAL. And, it has a pink seal on it clapping its fins." He rolls his whisky-colored eyes, but he's smiling.

Avery laughs. "Between the three of you, she's going to own a pink handgun by the time she's five."

"Probably," he says with a smile. "A girl needs to know how to protect herself. Especially if she gets in as much trouble as her mom."

They share a private look.

"I'd invite you to join us, but I get the feeling you already ate," Nick says.

"We did," Avery says. "But, thank you."

"Avery's obsessed with the cookies and cream milkshake here. Have you had it?" Ryker asks.

We shake our heads.

"Oh, my God, it's to die for," she gushes. "Smothered with Oreos, chocolate chip cookies, ice cream sandwiches, chocolate crunchies, frosting…"

"You're giving me a toothache," Nick says.

"I didn't think my sweet tooth could get any worse until I became pregnant," Avery says.

"It's okay, baby. You're eating for two." Ryker wraps his other arm around her waist and his hands move over her stomach. Avery laces her fingers through his and I can't help but smile. They are too adorable together.

"Well, it was good seeing you, Nick. And, nice meeting you, Savannah," Avery says. "I'm about ready to go back up to the room and put my swollen ankles up."

"C'mon, I'll take care of you, Ave," Ryker says. "Good meeting you."

Nick and I say goodbye and I watch them walk away. I know we've barely been married 24 hours, but I really want Nick to look at me the way Ryker looks at Avery.

One day, hopefully.

Chapter Twelve: Nick

When the plane touches down at LAX, it's back to the real world and I'm not going to lie. I'm a bit nervous about how people are going to react to our whirlwind wedding. When I tell Savannah we're going to my place first, she only shrugs.

I get the feeling she's annoyed with me. And, I'm thinking it's because I haven't told anyone we're married yet. But, hell, what am I supposed to do? Announce it to the world? It's nobody's damn business and I'm still trying to get used to the idea myself.

When we get to my place in Malibu, I roll our suitcases up and open the door. It doesn't look like much from the back where it sits on the edge of the Pacific Coast Highway, but once we step inside, I see Savannah's eyes widen.

"Oh, my gosh," she exclaims and walks over to the large, floor-to-ceiling windows that overlook the beach and Pacific Ocean. "Your house is literally on the beach. Like right on the freaking sand."

"I told you it was." I can't help but smile at her enthusiasm. She views everything with such delight and wide-eyed innocence. A true ingenue. I find that precious and so damn refreshing. Nothing was ever good enough for Margo and even the smallest thing seems to make Savannah smile.

"Well, yeah, but you could've been exaggerating." She presses her hands and nose to the window and I can't help but chuckle.

"C'mere," I say. I pull her over to a sliding door and show her the balcony. "I usually have my morning coffee out here."

The waves crash along the shore and the sun is bright against the blazing blue sky above. Savannah steps out and leans over the railing. "It's perfect," she says.

While she admires the ocean, I can't help but admire her. Those long, graceful limbs of hers remind me of a ballerina and I get the urge to pull her into my arms and kiss her. So, I do. Savannah wraps her arms around my neck and kisses me back, but I feel a distance in her response.

I pull back and study her. "What's wrong?"

She shrugs and turns her attention back to the ocean.

"Sav? I'm sorry if you're pissed about whatever happened earlier."

She turns back and I can see the hurt in her aqua eyes. "You didn't even introduce me. It's like I wasn't even there."

Shit, now I feel like a complete dick. "I'm sorry, sweetheart. I should have, but I'm still wrapping my head around everything. But, I promise I'll do better."

When she doesn't say anything, I lean down and capture her mouth in a long, heated kiss. And, the moment she melts into me, I know all is forgiven.

"What the hell is going on?" a voice hisses.

We both look over and Margo stands about ten feet away, hands on her hips, green eyes flashing. *Oh, shit, here we go,* I think. Savannah wanted an introduction and she's about to get one. Unfortunately, it's to Margo York.

"We didn't hear you come in," I say and glance down at the key in her hand.

"Apparently not." Her gaze slants to poor Savannah and shoots daggers.

I release Savannah and take a step back. "Margo, this is Savannah...my wife."

"What?" Her mouth drops and I can tell she's trying to process what I just said. Except, her brain is in complete denial.

"Hi," Savannah says in a small voice.

Margo ignores her and turns her full attention to me. "I'm sorry, I think I just hallucinated you saying this person is your wife."

"That's right." I reach for Savannah's hand. "We met this past weekend in Vegas and I know it's sudden, but-"

"Sudden?" she interrupts in a shrill voice. "Am I missing something here? I was practically your fiancée, Nicholas."

"We were never engaged. That was the problem, Margo. You never could seem to understand I didn't want to marry you."

"But, you married *her*?" She looks completely baffled and is beginning to sound a little whiny.

"I guess when the right one comes along, yeah."

Margo's face turns a deep, mottled shade of red and I swear I see smoke coming out of her ears. A part of me feels bad, but suddenly it becomes crystal clear to me that marrying her would've been the biggest mistake of my life. She's too selfish, too self-absorbed and too rich for my blood.

While Savannah, on the other hand, is kind, loving and views everything with a fresh, appreciative outlook.

If I have to suck it up and bite the bullet, I'd much rather spend my days and nights with Sav.

"Have you lost your mind?" Margo asks. "This has to be a joke. I refuse to believe anything else. I mean, really, Nicholas. Did you fall down, hit your little head and marry the first hooker you saw on the boulevard?"

I feel Savannah flinch and cast her an apologetic look. I knew an encounter with Margo was going to be bad, but she's being downright nasty. And, Savannah doesn't deserve to be treated like a whore. "Jealous, Margo?"

She forces a laugh. "You've got to be kidding." Finally, she turns her full attention to Savannah. Her gaze rakes down her and I squeeze Savannah's hand, wishing I could prepare her for the blast about to happen. "I don't know how you convinced him to marry you, but I'm sure it won't last. Whatever you're basing this farce of a marriage on, it'll grow old. He will get tired of you and leave you."

"Shut up, Margo," I hiss.

"You're an idiot," Margo snaps. "She could be your daughter." With a disgusted sound, Margo turns on her heel, slams the key down on a table and marches to the front door. She pulls it open then hits us with one more barb before she leaves. "Have fun with your child-bride. Are you sure she's even legal?"

After the door slams shut, Savannah pulls her hand out of mine. She looks a little stunned, like she's trying to process what just happened and I feel terrible. "I'm so sorry," I say.

"She was pleasant," Savannah says in a dry voice.

"Margo's a bitch. You didn't deserve that."

"How long were you two together?"

I let out a long breath. "A year."

"I'm sorry."

A half-laugh bubbles up within my throat. "It wasn't always horrible. But, lately, she's grown more and more unbearable. She was pressuring me to propose and gave me an ultimatum."

"But, you were considering it, right? I mean, you must've loved her at one point," Savannah says.

"I was never in love with Margo," I say. "I already told you-- I don't fall in love. And, if I would've married her, it would've been a marriage of convenience."

I know that sounds harsh, but it's the truth. Something flickers in Savannah's eyes.

"Is that why you married me? Convenience?"

"No offense, Sav, but I'm talking about money. Margo's family is worth half a billion dollars and I'm pretty sure yours isn't." I cock a brow. "Am I wrong?"

"My parents are retired school teachers."

I nod. "So, no, I didn't marry you for your money." Even though I try to make light of her question, Savannah isn't satisfied with the way I dodged it.

"What about us?' she asks. "Why did you dare me to marry you, Nick?"

It's actually a really good question, but one that I don't have a definitive answer to. "I don't know," I admit. When her face falls, I hurriedly add, "but I don't regret it." I take Savannah's hands in mine and search for those gorgeous blue eyes. "Please, believe me when I tell you it wasn't a mistake. I look forward to getting to know you and-" *falling in love with you?*

God, where did that even come from?

Because I don't do that. Ever. That would be breaking rule number one which would leave me vulnerable. *Not gonna happen.*

She raises a brow. "I just don't understand. Margo was trying to get you to propose for months probably. So, what possessed you to marry me after 24 hours?"

I suppose this might be a good time to mention my inheritance. Or, the fact that I was wildly attracted to her. Instead, I squeeze her hands and turn the question around on her. "I can ask you the exact same thing. After I was such a jerk to you, why did you agree to marry me?"

"Because I saw beneath that," she says without hesitation.

"What do you mean?"

She lays a hand against my chest, over my heart. "I saw inside. I glimpsed who you really are and it was...beautiful."

I'm not sure what she's referring to, but I appreciate the kind words. "You have a really good, pure soul, Savannah. That's what I saw."

"It doesn't hurt that you're not too shabby to look at either," she says with a grin.

"Not too shabby?" I yank her against me. "I'll show you shabby," I say and capture her mouth in a kiss. When there's a knock on the door, we pull apart.

"Do you think it's Margo again?" she asks.

"No, I bet it's Paul."

"Who's Paul?"

"Come find out," I say with a mysterious smile. I jog over and throw the door open. And, just like I thought, Noah stands there with a very clean Paul. I drop down, grab his big head in my hands and ruffle his fur. "Hey, there, boy. Good to see you again."

"He looks like a new dog, huh?" Noah asks. When he notices Savannah, his eyes widen a little in surprise.

"He certainly does," I say. "You got the money, okay?"

"Sure did. Thanks."

"Thanks for helping me with Paul."

"Any time. He's a good boy."

I say goodbye to Noah and lead Paul into the house. "Probably should take him out. Wanna come?" I ask Savannah and she nods enthusiastically.

We head down some stairs and I open the back door. We all step down onto the sand, I unleash Paul and he takes off like the happiest dog in the world. We follow him down to the water and watch as he frolics in the surf. "Beats the desert, huh, boy?" I ask him.

With a low whoof, Paul pounces through the water and Savannah and I laugh.

"I can't believe you brought him back and rescued him," she says, looking at me with bright eyes. "But, why in the world did you name him Paul?"

"You don't know?"

She shrugs. "No clue."

"His full name is Paul Maurice Marciano Knight."

Savannah bursts out laughing. "The founders of Guess? Oh, my gosh, that's hysterical."

We play on the beach with Paul and it's the best afternoon I've had in a long time. Savannah has an inner light that glows so bright. When she asked me why I dared her to marry me, I know that's one of the reasons. Maybe it sounds silly, but she has this inner beauty that shines so brightly. It draws me to her. Makes me want to get to know her better.

Get to know her thoroughly.

After romping around together for over an hour, the three of us go back inside. Back up in the living room, I feel a breeze and notice glass shards all over the floor. "Don't move," I tell her. "Here, hold Paul."

"What happened?" she asks, taking the dog's collar.

I wander over to the broken window by the front door and frown. "Someone broke the window." There's glass everywhere. "Stay there. I'm going to clean it up." It had to have been Margo. Who else would've done this? I wonder.

"Do you think it was Margo?" Savannah asks, reading my thoughts.

"Yeah. I wouldn't be surprised." While I sweep the glass up, I wonder what else Margo is capable of doing. After all, what's the saying? *A woman scorned…*

I dump the broken shards of glass into a garbage bag, pick up the brick that was used to break the window and take everything out to the trash. When I get back inside, I tell Savannah it might be a good idea to lay low for a few days. "Can we stay at your place?" I ask.

"Sure," she says. "As long as you don't mind a small apartment with a view of a pool instead of the ocean."

"I'll survive," I tell her.

Chapter Thirteen: Savannah

Nick drives us over to Sunset Terrace and I'd be lying if I said I wasn't nervous. My place is small and cozy. Not to mention, I have a lot of nosy neighbors who are going to be very curious when they see Nick.

We're also not allowed to have dogs so I'm really hoping to avoid Ryan Fox, the owner and building manager. He lives in the corner unit and has always been very nice to me, but I don't think it would be good if he saw us sneaking Paul into my place.

Although, it's inevitable.

My apartment is the middle one, directly facing the pool where everyone gathers, and Ryan is always out and about, fixing things and keeping his eye on the property.

Nick and I don't pull up until after dark, so I'm hoping luck is on our side. He parks his Dodge in the street since my car is in the spot behind the building and while he gathers his stuff out of the trunk, I take Paul's leash.

I told Nick that I couldn't have dogs so we sneak up the walkway as quietly as possible and the coast looks clear. No one is at the pool and I let out a sigh of relief. "C'mon," I say and motion him to follow me.

Halfway to my door, Ryan Fox turns the corner. *Damn.*

His dark eyes widen and I'm not sure if it's more because of Nick or the dog. I don't know a lot about Ryan except what I hear the other girls say-- he's in his early 40s, divorced, a former military pilot and we call him Foxy Flyboy. Every time I see him, he always says hello and gives a polite wave, but there's no missing the sadness in his eyes.

"Hi, Savannah," he says and glances over at Nick. It's like he doesn't even notice the furry, panting dog. "Everything okay?"

I hear the concern in his voice. Unlike the other tenants, I've never brought anyone home with me before and I don't think Ryan expects to see an older man like Nick heading into my place with me. "Yeah, everything is great. Just finished up a shoot in Vegas. How are you?"

"Fine, thanks."

The air fills with an awkward pause.

"Oh, Ryan this is Nick," I say, my throat dry and closing up. "Nick, this is my landlord, Ryan Fox."

They both nod and mumble a greeting, but it's extremely uncomfortable. I almost feel like they're sizing each other up which makes no sense.

"I fixed your sink disposal," Ryan says.

"Great. Well, see you around," I say and slip my key into the door.

"If it starts acting up again just let me know."

"Will do." I push the door open.

"Uh, Savannah?"

I stifle a sigh and turn back to Ryan. "Yes?"

"Your friend isn't, ah, staying permanently, right?"

The way he says it, it's hard to tell whether he's asking about Nick or the dog. "Sorry, no. Just a few days, if that's okay?"

"Sure," Ryan says, still eyeing Nick.

"Thanks, Ryan." When I see Nick's eyes start to narrow at Ryan, I grab his hand and tug him inside.

After I close and lock the door, Nick crosses his arms. "What the hell was that guy's problem?"

"He's just protective of the girls here. Kinda like a father figure. He's never seen me bring a man home so it probably caught him off-guard. He's actually a really nice guy."

"I'm sure."

His voice drips with sarcasm. "What's that supposed to mean?"

"The guy needs to mind his own business. And, for someone who's so keen on being introduced, you kind of stumbled through that."

"What are you talking about?"

"Why didn't you tell him the truth? That I'm your husband."

I unleash Paul and know Nick's right. It crossed my mind to introduce him as my husband, say that I got married, but for the first time, I understand what Nick felt earlier when the situation was reversed. The whole thing feels a little strange still.

"I'm sorry. You're right. But, don't be mad at Ryan. He's actually very sweet."

"Sweet?" Nick makes a face. "C'mon, Sav. Guys aren't sweet unless they want something." Nick takes a step closer, silver-gray eyes flashing. "Did he ever hit on you?"

"No!" I burst out laughing.

"What's so funny?"

I realize I'm about to say he's way too old for me then bite my lip. He and Nick are probably the same age. "Nothing. He's just...harmless."

But, Nick shakes his head. "No, I saw the way he looked at you. It was far from harmless."

I've never heard Nick sound jealous. But, there is no denying it. He's positively green with envy over Foxy Flyboy. I chew my lower lip, trying to hide my smile and I think it just makes Nick more mad.

"You think this is funny?" Nick demands.

"I didn't think you were the jealous type."

His nostrils flare and he checks his emotions. "I'm not," he says. Then, his arm snaps out and he pulls me against him. "But, you make me a little crazy," he growls and slams his mouth down against mine.

Nick holds me tight, almost too tight, and he pushes his tongue between my lips, kissing me in a way he hasn't before. It's fast, hard, demanding and totally unexpected.

And, I like it. A lot.

I wind my arms around his neck and he slides his hands over my rear-end and scoops me up. I wrap my legs around his waist and he pulls his mouth free and looks around, breathing hard. "Where's your room?"

"That way," I say.

Nick carries me down the hall and into my bedroom, pries me off and tosses me onto the bed. He pulls his shirt over his head and then starts to work his jeans off. There's a savage look in his eye and the slow, gentleman from the other night is nowhere to be found.

Heat gathers low in my stomach as I watch him.

"Take your clothes off," he says, now only in his boxer briefs. Then, he heads back into the other room.

My heart thunders at the order. I've never seen this predatory, almost feral side of him before, and I'm not going to lie. It's turning me on and I'm a little scared. But, in a good way. My blood is pumping hard as I slide off the bed and take my t-shirt and capris off.

When Nick returns, he kicks the door shut and tosses a few condoms on the nightstand. His gaze runs over me, still in my bra and underwear. "Why aren't you naked yet?"

I swallow hard. "Maybe I was hoping you'd help me."

Heat flares in his eyes. He stalks over, slides my bra straps down my arms and dips his head to swirl his tongue from the top of one breast to the other. "I'm not feeling especially patient tonight, Savannah," he warns me and I feel a nip through my satin bra.

I gasp, arch into his chest and slide my fingers through his hair. Then, his long fingers trail down my sides and hook into the top of my panties. He yanks them down and I let out a surprised sound. His hand drops between us and when he cups me, my body jerks at the intimate touch. "You are all mine and this belongs to me," he whispers, eyes flashing. "Say it. Tell me you're mine."

"I'm yours," I whisper.

"Don't ever forget it."

God. When he begins stroking me, my legs turn to jelly, and Nick scoops me up with a curse. He lays me out on the bed, then drops down at the edge of the mattress and drags me closer, returning his attention back to below my waist. I bite my lip when he slides a finger inside me. Then, his dark head drops between my thighs and I bite the inside of my cheek as his mouth begins to suck and lick.

"Nick," I moan. God, he's really too good at this and I try to squeeze my thighs together, fighting the overwhelming sensations that seem to be pushing me right to the edge of a precipice.

But, he's not having it and shoves his hands under my ass, lifts me right up off the mattress and buries his face between my legs. I gasp, dig my nails into the bedspread and feel totally out of control.

It's clear that Nick is the one in control right now.

Whatever precipice I'm hovering at, I tip over the moment he pulls my throbbing bud between his lips and sucks. A cry tears from my mouth and waves of pleasure roll through my lower body. Nick slides up onto the bed, moving up my body and pulls my bra the rest of the way off.

Lying naked beneath him, panting hard, I push my pelvis up against him, wanting to feel him inside me again. His lip curls up in a smirk and he grinds his hardness against my wet center.

"Something you want, sweetheart?"

"Yes," I pant. "Please."

"And, what's that?" he asks and licks up the side of my face.

Feeling hesitant, I reach down and lay my hand over the front of his boxer briefs. *He's so hard.* I run my fingers down then back up in a feather-like caress. Nick groans then pushes back, yanks the boxer briefs off and reaches for a condom.

"Wait," I say.

"Baby, I can't wait."

"But, I want to...get to know you better," I say in a low voice. I'm scared he's going to ignore my request, but he freezes.

"Okaaay." He swallows hard and watches closely as I reach back down and wrap my fingers around his long, hard length. His eyes slide shut. "Jesus," he hisses and his hips jerks.

When I start to move my hand up then down, slowly stroking him, he grits his teeth, struggling to stay up on his elbows, muscles flexing. "Is this okay?" I ask.

"Harder," he says, his voice scratchy.

When I comply, his breathing begins to sound all harsh and raspy and I watch, fascinated as he struggles for control. "*Fuck. Stop*," he hisses.

With a shaky hand, he rips the packet open, rolls the condom on and lines himself up with my center. Unlike last night, Nick's control hangs by a thread and when he grips my hips and squeezes hard, I prepare myself.

Nick plunges into me and I arch my back and cry out.

"Are you okay?" he asks, pausing.

I nod, adjusting to his size, trying to get comfortable.

"Relax," he murmurs and begins to move, rocking his hips, pulling me with him. I let my legs fall open, wrap my ankles around his calves, and meet his thrusts. Tonight is harder, faster and rougher, but there's an excitement to it.

Nick reaches his hand down where we're joined and begins to massage me. Pretty soon, I'm writhing, bucking up beneath him, and when he pushes down with his thumb just right, it's like *ding, ding, ding!* Like lights and bells going off on a winning slot machine and the coins begin to fall.

I think I scream his name, but I'm so lost in such intense waves of pleasure that I can't be sure. Above me, Nick shudders hard and groans. He rolls over and drops down on the pillow beside me, breathing hard, a hand on his chest, the other thrown over his head. "Jesus Christ, Sav."

For a long moment, we just lay there, dazed. Then, I feel him tilt his head and look over. I meet his intense gray gaze and neither of us says a word.

But, we communicate something.

A shiver runs through me and finally Nick looks away. He pads off to the bathroom to dispose of the condom and when he returns, he helps me pull the covers back. Then, he gathers me against his chest, presses a kiss to my hairline and I snuggle down into his arms and fall asleep.

Chapter Fourteen: Nick

The next morning, Savannah and I take a leisurely walk around the neighborhood with Paul. We grab coffees at the corner shop and enjoy the sunshine as we wander with no destination in mind, just enjoying each other's company.

I toss my cup after I finish the caffeine and reach for Savannah's hand. I love the feel of her slim fingers tangled in mine and we pause while Paul sniffs a tree. *Mine.* I look down and study Savannah. Her blonde hair glitters like gold in a ray of sunlight and when she glances up at me, her aqua eyes resemble two clear pools of water. And, all I want to do is drown in their depths.

I've never been much of a romantic, but something in me is changing. I get the feeling Savannah is turning me into a damn sap. And, I don't even care. That doesn't mean I'm developing feelings for her, though, I tell myself.

Even though, deep down, I can feel the tide turning. And, if I'm not careful, I know there's the possibility that it could suck me under and drown me.

"Was I-- too rough last night?" I ask her. It's been on my mind since I woke up and I didn't get the impression that I hurt her, but she's so new to being intimate with a man.

"No. I mean, I am a little sore, but it's like a good feeling."

Dammit, I should've slowed down and taken more time. "Sore feels good?" I ask, upset with myself for being too fast with her.

"When it still feels like you're inside me...yes, it's a good thing."

Heat slams through me and I pull her close, kissing her like no one else is around. Like we aren't standing in the middle of a public sidewalk. God, I love the feel of her full, soft lips and the way her mouth opens to mine. She tastes like vanilla and sugar, just how she flavored her coffee, and I want to devour her.

Instead, I remind myself that people are nearby, and break my mouth away. "Let's go back," I whisper. I lace my fingers through hers again and guide her and Paul back to the apartment. The second we're inside, I drop the dog's leash and haul Savannah up against me, dropping kisses all over her face and neck.

I don't know what's wrong with me, but I can't get enough of her.

She lets out a breathy laugh and tilts her head to give me better access. When her phone rings, I'm reluctant to let her go. "Nick," she giggles and pushes a hand against my chest.

"Ignore it," I growl and suck on the sensitive curve where her neck and shoulder meet.

"It could be about work."

I let out a frustrated sigh and step back while she leans over and swipes her phone off the coffee table. There are so many things I still want to teach her and my mind begins to conjure up all the positions and places we've yet to experience. I plan to take her all over this apartment and then when we move into my place permanently, we're going to christen every room, every piece of furniture and then I'm going to fuck her in the ocean under the moonlight.

I try to tamp down my dirty thoughts and focus on her conversation. But, when I watch her glossy, pink lips move when she talks, I'm picturing them wrapped around my cock.

"That's amazing!" she exclaims, eyes bright. "Yes, I know who he is…"

He? I wonder who she's talking about. From what I can hear, she's definitely talking to her agent. Maybe they have some news about the pictures we just took in Vegas. I haven't heard anything yet from the client, but I know the shots turned out amazing and, if they're smart, they'll hire Savannah to be in their next ten campaigns.

"It is a dream come true. Yes, for sure. Okay, sounds good. Bye."

After she hangs up, she squeals and jumps up and down. I can't help but smile at her zest for life. It's contagious. Before Savannah, I was unhappy and moody a lot of the time. But, now, with her carefree positivity surrounding me, it's beginning to rub off.

"What's got you so happy, sweetheart?"

"That was my agent. Guess is thrilled with the pictures we took."

"I knew they would be," I say and my smile widens.

"They're so happy that they want me to be the face of a new line they're launching."

"That's terrific," I say and swoop her into my arms. "I'm so proud of you."

"And, that's not all. I get to go to Capri! That's where they're shooting. Two weeks in Italy, can you believe it?"

"Capri?" My smile wilts. I don't want Savannah to leave for two weeks. I mean, I suppose I could go with her and we could make a honeymoon of it between her time working.

"Yes! And, the model I'll be working with is Simon LaFleur. He's like only *the* biggest model right now!"

What little is left of my smile dissolves completely. "Simon LaFleur?" I groan. I don't even have the words to describe what a creep and a playboy he is on set. Everyone knows it.

"Have you worked with him?" she asks.

"No, but I know all about how he seduces every model he works with and is a complete cocksman."

"Well, luckily, I'm a married woman."

Even though she's teasing, I'm not happy. "You don't have to do it. You can retire right now."

She looks a little taken aback by my words. "Retire already?" She shakes her head. "I told you my plan. Model, save some money and go to school."

"Plans change. Why not just go to school now? I'll pay for it." *As soon as I get my hands on that inheritance,* I think.

"I appreciate that, Nick, but I don't want to be completely dependent on you. I want to make my own money and contribute, too."

I know I'm being irrational and should be happy for her, but the idea that she'll be working with that prick Simon makes my skin crawl. He's going to take one look at Savannah and be all over her. Just as I'm about to tell her that, my phone rings.

I glance down at the caller i.d. and sigh. "Hi, Mom," I say. I figure it's about time I let her know what's happening, but I don't want to do it over the phone. "No, I'm fine. Just, ah, got a lot on my mind."

I figure the best way to break the news about Margo and Savannah is in person with both my parents and I suggest dinner. I'm not expecting her to want to do it tonight, but she does. "Is that okay?" she asks.

"Dinner tonight?" I repeat, looking at Savannah. She nods. "Yeah, sure. I'm going to be bringing someone with me, too. No, not Margo. Look, I'll explain everything when I see you and John later, okay?"

After I hang up, I sigh. "Well, this should be interesting."

"I'm nervous," she says and wraps her arms around her middle.

"Don't be. Once they get over the initial shock, they're going to love you."

I just never would have predicted how much.

When we get to my parents' place in Simi Valley, I take Savannah's hand and halfway up the walkway, my Mom throws the front door open. "Hi, Mom," I say and give her a hug and kiss on the cheek. My stepdad is right behind her and he claps me on the back as we embrace.

We step into the foyer and I see the curious looks when I reach over and take Savannah's hand again. "Mom, John, this is Savannah...my wife."

Both of their eyes look about to bulge out of their skulls.

"Well, this is unexpected news," my Mom says, always polite. "But, it's so nice to meet you. I'm Judy."

"It's nice to meet you, too," Savannah says.

"Last I knew, you had a fiancée, Nick," my step dad says. "Margo something or other?" Leave it to John. He's never one to mince words.

"John," my mom scolds. "They're barely in the door. Why don't you go get us all a glass of wine and we can sit down and let them tell us what happened."

Once we're all seated in the living room and I suck down half my wine in one gulp, I tell my parents that Margo and I broke up last week. I let them know I hadn't been happy in a long time and when she gave me an ultimatum, I broke it off.

"No big loss there," John comments in a dry voice.

"It's probably for the best," Mom says. "She wasn't ever very friendly."

"Right after we broke up, I left for a shoot in Vegas where I met Savannah on set."

"Oh, you worked together?"

"Never smart to mix business with pleasure, Nick," John says.

"Well, it was this time around," I tell them and squeeze Savannah's hand.

"How did a photo shoot lead to marriage?" my mom asks as delicately as possible. "Seems a little sudden. No offense, dear," she adds and glances at Savannah.

"That's actually a good question," Savannah says.

Savannah looks up at me. "Completely understandable," I say, agreeing with them both. Yet, I don't offer an answer.

"How old are you?" John asks out of the blue.

Savannah shifts on the couch. "Twenty-one."

"Twenty-one?" he asks in disbelief. "For chrissake, Nick, she could be your-"

"Daughter. Yeah, I know, but thanks for pointing that out."

"Well, I never put too much emphasis on age," my mom says. "The important thing is that you're both on the same page. A successful marriage relies on mutual respect, the ability to compromise, honesty and, of course, love. I may not have understood that the first time around, but I know now." She and John share a smile.

"It *was* sudden," Savannah says, "but we just knew. Maybe it should've felt strange, but it didn't."

When my parents look at me, I just shrug. "When you know, you know."

"Good news is you got rid of that lousy Margaret," John says.

"Margo. And, yeah, I dodged a bullet."

After a few more questions, we walk over to the table to eat. Savannah sits next to me and my mom is on her other side. As we fill our plates with my mom's cooking, Savannah says, "Nick tells me how much he loves your macaroni and cheese. I'd really like to get the recipe, if that's okay?"

My mom's eyes light up. Compliment her cooking and you've won her over for life. "Of course. After dinner, I'll write it down for you."

"Thank you," Savannah says.

While my mom chats Savannah up between bites, I'm glad things are going well. They seem to like her and who wouldn't? Savannah is polite and sweet. I honestly don't think she has a mean bone in her body. And, her bright attitude and overall happiness is contagious. I used to always get so easily annoyed and snappy. My moodiness was renowned. But, now, nothing is bothering me.

Well, except for Savannah possibly working with Simon LaFleur in Capri.

But, right now, I just sit back, sip my wine and watch Savannah charm my parents. By the end of the meal, she has them wrapped around her finger and they're laughing and sharing stories like old friends.

We go back into the living room and my mom pulls Savannah over to the couch to sit down next to her. "You should've seen him," my mom says and looks over at me. "He used to wear my blue tights, a red shirt and snow boots. Then, he'd pretend he was Superman and start running around the house saying he was flying."

"That's how he tripped and fell down the steps. Broke his front teeth right out," my stepdad adds and they all laugh. "Took two years until his adult teeth finally came in."

"I'm glad you all find that story so amusing."

"You wore your Mom's tights?" Savannah asks and covers her mouth to stifle the giggles.

"I wanted to be Superman. Leave me alone." But, the grumpiness in my voice isn't genuine.

After another hour of humiliating childhood stories about me, I stand up and stretch. "That's about all my ego can take," I say. "Besides, we have to get back and let the dog out."

"Dog?" John echoes in disbelief.

"You got a dog?" my mom asks, voice full of wonder.

Shit. I see her eyes glisten with tears. "Yes, Mom," I say and pull her in for a goodbye hug. God, I hate when she cries. "I'm on my way to being domesticated."

She hugs me tightly and then, under her breath, says, "Grandma would be so happy."

Yeah, I have a feeling that my feisty, eccentric Grandma would've loved Savannah just as much as they do.

"Be good to her, Nick," my mom whispers. "And, get to work on some grandchildren for me."

Oh, Lord. I say goodbye, take Savannah's hand and pull her out of there before they name our first born without me.

Later that night, Savannah and I curl up on the couch with a bottle of wine and Paul snoring at our feet. It's a perfect night, the patio doors are wide open and the warm ocean breeze blows inside. When I glance down at Savannah, she leans in and presses a kiss to my shoulder.

"I heard your mom's comment," she says and I merely raise a brow. "About grandchildren." When I don't say anything, she pulls back and looks at me closely. "How do you feel about kids?"

"Why do I feel a game of Questions & Secrets coming on?"

"Because there's still so much I want to know about you."

She waits for me to answer. *Stubborn thing.* "What was the question again?"

Savannah slugs me in the arm.

"Okay, okay. Honestly, I've never given it much thought. I've always taken precautions to make sure it doesn't happen."

"So, you don't want kids?"

"I didn't say that."

"You're avoiding the question."

I let out a sigh and know that she's right. "I'm an only child so I never grew up with a bunch of siblings. And, my dad took off when I was really young, so for me, family was just my mom, my grandma and John. And, my grandma died last year…" My voice trails off lamely. "I'm sorry, I know this isn't answering your question and I'm talking in circles because I have no idea if I want children. I question if I would even be a good dad. I didn't have the greatest role model, you know."

"But, you had John."

"True and I'm grateful for that, but my real father was a piece of shit. He didn't love anybody but himself. He was selfish, arrogant-"

Oh, my God. It hits me hard, completely out of the blue, that I could be describing myself. "Is that what you see?" I ask her. "When you look at me?"

Suddenly, I need to know. *Am I just as bad as my dad?*

Savannah turns and grasps my hands in hers. "No, of course not. I wouldn't have married you." She gives my hands a reassuring squeeze and then looks at me with that sweet, shy smile of hers. "I think you would be an amazing father."

"Really? Why?"

"Because you're a good man, Nick. With a good heart. If you don't believe me, just ask Paul," she says and leans down to pet the sleepy mongrel. "Isn't he a good Daddy? Rescuing you from that desert?"

Half asleep, Paul makes a half bark-half growl sound in the back of his throat and we both laugh.

"I know you'd be a wonderful mother," I tell her.

"Thank you. Not that there's any rush," she adds. "Most couples probably talk about this kind of thing before they get married so I just wondered where you stood."

"I stand by you," I say.

A smile curves her mouth. "Any preference?" she asks.

"What do you mean?"

"Boy or girl, silly," she says.

"Oh! Wow, you do have babies on the brain," I tease and grab her sides, tickling her.

Savannah squeals and twists away. "I'm just curious. We never got to talk about any of this because we never actually dated."

I let out a sigh. "I have this weird feeling that I'd have a daughter."

"Really? Why?"

"Because God's going to punish me for my wild, younger days."

"Hmm. Maybe you deserve it."

"Probably," I acknowledge.

"And, if your daughter came home one day with a husband who was 21 years older than her-"

I raise a hand. "No. Please, don't."

"Nick!"

I groan and decide I don't ever want to meet Savannah's father. Whatever shit he may give me, it's going to be well-deserved. "Promise me that we will only have boys."

Savannah laughs. "They say boys are easier but I've always thought it would be nice to have a little girl."

"Then, promise me that if we ever have a daughter, she will not be allowed to date until she's 18."

"Good luck enforcing that rule," she says with a smirk.

"Trust me when I say I will do everything in my power to discourage any potential suitors."

For a moment, neither of us says anything and I think back to when we ran into Avery and Ryker at the restaurant in Las Vegas. They were positively glowing and looked so prepared to be parents. I imagine I'd be the complete opposite. Completely frazzled and unprepared.

But, I guess that's just a part of the learning curve.

I have a feeling that Savannah and I aren't going to be the kind of couple who take the traditional path in life. So far, neither of us has-- we became models which isn't your run-of-the-mill, average career choice and then we eloped at a cheesy Vegas chapel when we barely knew each other.

Yeah, with the way things are going, I wouldn't be surprised if Savannah was knocked up in a week with triplets.

Oh, God, I don't even want to put that energy out in the Universe. My luck, it would be three little girls.

Honestly, though, it would be kind of cute having three mini Savannah's running around this place. I pull her into the crook of my arm and press a kiss to the top of her head. "Sav? By any chance do triplets run in your family?"

Savannah pulls back and looks up at me with wide, blue eyes. "No!" she exclaims with a laugh. "Why?"

"No reason," I murmur and pull her back down into my arms. "Want to watch another movie?"

"Sure. As long as it's a scary one."

I chuckle and pull up an all-horror streaming service that we constantly watch.

"Nick?"

"Hmm?"

"Not to freak you out or anything, but my Grandma has a twin. And, her cousin had a twin. And, it usually skips-"

"A generation," I finish.

I suck in a breath and Savannah stifles a laugh against my shoulder. "And, you were worried about one girl," she says. "Silly man."

Twin girls.

Hell, at this rate, I wouldn't be surprised.

Chapter Fifteen: Savannah

The week flies by and I spend most of it in Nick's arms--tasting his kiss, feeling his touch and getting lost in those silvery metallic eyes. The more time I spend with him, the more attached I feel myself becoming. He's stirring up emotions in me that I never felt before.

I've never been in a relationship with a man before and I enjoy every moment in Nick's company. He makes me laugh all the time whether he means to or not and the way he looks at me makes me feel protected and secure.

We've been married for just over a week and it feels like I've known him forever. I truly can't imagine my life without him. I try not to think about it too hard, but in the back of my mind, I know I'm falling in love with him.

I guess it was bound to happen sooner or later, but I'm just nervous because I remember his words only too clearly: *"I don't fall in love, Savannah. It makes you vulnerable and miserable when things eventually don't work out. Because, trust me, they never do."*

Despite his jaded words, he seems to enjoy my company and our long conversations where we just lay in bed or on the couch and spend time getting to know each other better. I call it our "Questions and Secrets" game because we can ask each other anything and we usually end up learning a lot of little things-- favorite things, likes and dislikes.

And, let's be honest, I may not be that experienced in the bedroom, but I know he enjoys the sex. Thoroughly. He's a very good teacher and he tells me I'm a very good student. There are still quite a few things I want to try, though, and I know he loves hearing that.

Love.

I wish I could hear what he's thinking. He's always thoughtful and tender, but love is an entirely different animal. To me, love is the end all, be all. It's more than just butterflies and infatuation. It's deeper and more intense. A feeling that rocks your formerly stable world to its core. Love is someone that I can't live without. Someone I'd die for.

And, right now, I'm falling head over heels in love with Nick Knight.

I'm falling in love with my husband.

Maybe we did things a little backwards, put the cart before the horse as my mom likes to say, but eventually we're going to end up at the same destination. We just took a bit of a different path to get there. To get to our forever.

And, some people might think I'm being overly optimistic and a little naive, but I believe in the power of love. I believe in Nick and me. I'm really hoping that with some more time, I'll be able to make him see that life can be a fairytale.

It's the Fourth of July and every year the residents of Sunset Terrace have a big barbeque and get-together around the pool. I just finished making a big bowl of potato salad to bring and, as I cover it with some aluminum foil, I hear Nick wander up behind me and slide his arms around my waist. When he begins to kiss my neck, I lean back in his arms and sigh.

I believe in Nick and me. I really, really do.

"Maybe we should skip this thing and just go straight to bed," he murmurs between kisses.

"Nick," I say and squirm away. "I want you to meet my friends." All week, it's been quiet around here because everyone was traveling for work. But, now, because of the holiday, they should be back and I'm looking forward to showing my man off.

He sighs. "I know, I know. I just thought I'd try to tempt you into a night of extreme pleasure-"

"Stop it," I say, unable to miss the heated look rising in his eyes. "Let me just change into my bathing suit and we can go."

"Can I watch?"

I laugh. "No! Stay put," I order him and hurry away. I toss a flirty look over my shoulder. "You're becoming a very bad influence on me, you know that?"

"I hope so."

Five minutes later, we walk across the yard with Paul and it looks like the whole crew is here. Jazz is the only one who knows about Nick because we talked over the phone. She just returned from a fashion show in Milan and I know she's dying to meet him.

The moment we appear, Jasmine sweeps over, all elegant-looking in a sheer cover-up, chunky jewelry and gold sandals. She wears full makeup and it's quite clear she has no intention of actually going swimming. "Savvy!" She calls and then gives me a hug. "Nick, I'm not sure if you remember, but we worked together before." She shakes his hand, eyeing him up and down.

"I remember. Good to see you, Jasmine," he says. "I heard you're doing a lot of runway now."

"That's right. I'm Savannah's next door neighbor who's been trying to get her to go out and live life for the past year. Guess it just took meeting you to bring out her wild and crazy side."

Taylor, my other neighbor, appears. Normally, her long red hair is pulled back into a tight, low bun, but tonight it hangs loosely around her face. "Well, if it isn't the two lovebirds." She studies Nick then bumps me with an elbow. "Good job, Savvy."

Maybe Jasmine isn't the only one who knows about our marriage, after all.

I can feel my face turn red as I introduce Nick. "Taylor is a ballerina," I tell him.

"Classically-trained and aspiring ballerina by day, hip-hop dancer by night," she says and does a little pirouette.

Nick smiles. "Nice to meet you."

"Better put your order in over at the grill with Foxy Flyboy," Jasmine says.

"Does he know you guys call him that?" Nick asks.

The girls all laugh.

"No way," Taylor says.

"And, even if he did, he's too polite to say anything," Jasmine adds.

"What do you want?" I ask Nick. "Burger or hotdog?"

"I'll take a burger."

"Okay. Be right back." I walk over to set the potato salad on a table and say hi to Ryan and put our order in.

Ryan eyes me as he adds another patty and hot dog on the grill while I grab a couple of beers from the cooler. "So, ah, I hear you tied the knot?"

Jazz has such a big mouth, I think. "Yeah, um, last week." I guess at this point, I should just assume everyone knows.

"And, how long have you known this guy?"

"Nick and I met while working in Vegas."

He arches a dark brow. For a moment he doesn't say anything. "Well, for what it's worth, you seem really happy. So, congrats."

"Thanks, Ryan. I appreciate it."

As I walk away, I glance back over my shoulder and can't help but notice the sadness that always seems to hover around Ryan. I know his marriage didn't work out and he's been divorced for years. And, in all the time I've lived here, he's never mentioned a date or brought a woman back home.

I get the feeling that Foxy Flyboy is a very lonely man. In a way, he kind of reminds me of how I was a week ago. He rarely goes out, just spends his days putzing around the building. I hope he finds someone like I did because I'd love to see a smile on his handsome face for once.

Just when I think things are going well, Cody and Mason come downstairs. The dynamic duo, as we like to call them, spend most of their time at the beach. Both are pro-surfers and travel all around the world competing in various competitions. They're extremely tan, well-built and like to drink and flirt.

When they see Nick sitting next to me, I notice them exchange a look. "Brother visiting, Savannah?" Cody asks with a smirk.

"She doesn't have a brother," Nick says in a nonchalant voice.

"Cody, Mason, this is Nick, my-"

"Her husband!" Jasmine gushes. "Eat your heart out boys. This is what a real man looks like."

"Aww, what the hell do you know, Jazz? You only date pussies." Cody elbows Mason, but he doesn't say anything.

I feel kind of bad because when Mason asked me out last year, I said no and brushed him off with some excuse. Now, he's looking from me to Nick like a puppy dog who just got kicked.

"Are we allowed to have dogs now?" Cody asks, eyeing Paul.

"No," Ryan immediately pipes in from over by the grill. "Paul is just visiting for a bit."

"Paul, huh?" Cody scratches him behind the ear. Paul leans into his hand and looks like he's smiling.

"How was Hawaii, fellas?" Taylor asks.

Cody gives the hang loose/ shaka hand sign and grins. "Massive waves, right, brah?" He turns to Mason and slaps his back. "Mase here caught a huge one. It was stellar."

"Yeah," Mason finally smiles. "It was pretty amazing once I knew I wasn't going to die."

We all laugh and then Ryan calls out that the food is ready. Everyone fills their plates and we sit around the pool and just talk. Jasmine tells us about her show in Milan, the guys share some funny stories about their trip to Hawaii and then everyone looks at us.

"The Guess shoot was…" I look over at Nick and smile. "Well, a dream come true. It was all a whirlwind and what happened between us was sudden, but I've never been happier."

"Then, we're happy for you," Mason says. I appreciate how sincere and grown-up he's being about the situation.

"Thank you, Mason," I say and give him a little smile.

Congratulations fill the air and a moment later I see Morgan heading over. I'm assuming she worked late again. Probably picked up an extra shift to help pay some of her mom's hospital bills. With her brown hair and blue eyes, Morgan is a natural beauty. She doesn't need to pile on the makeup or dress skimpy to get a man's attention. I wish she'd catch a break with acting, but as more time passes, her dream seems to be fading away.

"Hey, guys," she says and pulls up a chair. Up close, I immediately notice the dark circles under her eyes and it looks like she may have been crying earlier. I feel bad that her mom is so sick. We all do.

Ryan hands her a plate with a hotdog. "Eat up, kid. Looks like you haven't had a bite in days."

"Thank you," she says.

As the afternoon goes on, some people jump in the pool while others sit around and catch up on each other's lives. While Mason and Cody take turns doing cannonballs into the deep end, the girls and I sit in lounge chairs and chat. Nearby, Nick seems to be making friends with Ryan.

"Looks like Foxy Flyboy might have found a new friend, y'all," Jasmine says.

"God knows he needs one," Taylor adds. "The man never leaves this complex. If I didn't know better, I'd say he's cursed and stuck here or something."

"So, what's he like?" Jasmine asks me in a low voice, waggling her perfect eyebrows. "Last time I saw you, Savannah Hart, you were a quiet, little virgin. And, now you're married to a hottie."

"That's Savannah Knight now, thank you very much. And, I've never been one to kiss and tell-"

"Because you never did any kissing," Taylor interrupts.

"Look who's talking," I say and Taylor just shrugs. Like me, Morgan and Taylor never have boyfriends.

"I bet she's doing more than kissing now," Morgan says, eyeing Nick. "He looks...demanding."

They all burst into laughter and Nick and Ryan glance over.

"Let's just say I've learned quite a few things and I have no complaints when it comes to that."

"We want details," Jasmine cries.

My face flushes and I adjust my sunglasses. "He's...perfect. In every way."

"Now that sounds like a lady who's satisfied," Taylor says with a smirk. "Does he have any single friends? And, I don't care how old they are!"

"Right?" Morgan adds. "Maybe we all need to find ourselves an older man."

"Dibs on Foxy Flyboy," Taylor says and we all die laughing.

"Actually," I say in a low voice, "I need some advice."

"Bedroom advice?" Jazz asks with a smirk and I nod.

"Well, don't look at me," Taylor says.

"Or, me," Morgan adds. "That's why Jazz is here."

"Well, Nick is very, ah, dominant in the bedroom."

"Can't say I'm surprised," Jasmine says. "He's a total alpha male used to bossing people around all day on set."

"Right. But, I kind of want to surprise him and shake things up instead of being so submissive all the time."

"Have you given him a blow job yet?" Jazz asks.

I shake my head.

Jasmine gives me a wicked smile. "If you want him to lose his shit and control then here's what you need to do…"

All four of us huddle together and the advice she gives makes my face turn bright red. Morgan and Taylor also look a little flushed.

"After that X-rated description, I need to go cool off," Taylor announces.

"Me, too," Morgan adds.

Jazz sits at the edge and dips her long legs while Taylor, Morgan and I go into the pool. As I float around on my back, I think over the past week and can't believe how everything has changed so much. I'm married to Nick Knight. It's still surreal. Honestly, I don't know when or if it will ever feel normal.

I pull myself up, treading water, and feel Nick's gaze. When I glance over where he sits with Ryan, drinking a beer, my heart stutters. The steamy look he's sending my way is quite clear and despite the cool water, a warmth saturates my blood.

When the sun starts to set, everyone begins to go their separate ways and I wave goodbye to Jazz and Taylor, the only two still outside. "Good luck," Jazz mouths and I feel my face burn red all over again.

Nick and I wander back to the apartment, Paul's leash in my hand. The moment the door closes, Nick drags me over and kisses me senseless.

"I've been wanting to do that for hours," he says. "Since the moment you took that coverup off and pranced around in that little bikini of yours."

"I hardly pranced," I say.

"You pranced," he confirms, running his hands down my hips and over my backside. When he squeezes, I drop my head back, fully expecting to feel his lips press kisses along my neck. But, instead, he releases me and takes a step back. "Take the coverup off," he says.

I lick my lips and slowly pull the cotton dress over my head. Even though I still wear my bathing suit, I feel completely exposed before his devouring eyes.

"I want you to pose for me," he says and reaches for his camera. "Without the bathing suit."

I suck in a breath.

Oh. My. God.

"Nick-"

"Stop talking and get undressed."

His voice is raspy and, at first, I'm unsure. "Here?" I ask.

"Wherever I say. I'm the photographer. And you, sweetheart, are the model whose job is to do whatever I demand."

I swallow hard, reach behind me and untie the strings. Nick holds out his hand and I place my top in his palm. He tosses it and lifts the camera. "Up against the wall," he says.

I follow his direction, my heart thundering in my ears, and lay my palms flat against the wall. I tip my head, arch my back and instantly I'm in model-mode. The camera starts snapping and I flow from one pose to the next, while Nick gives direction.

"So fucking beautiful," he murmurs.

After another minute, he nods toward the bedroom. "C'mon. Before I rip those bottoms off and fuck you up against that wall."

My eyes widen and I scurry into the other room. Nick follows me, a predatory look in his eye, and kicks the door shut. "On the bed," he says.

As I scoot back on the mattress, I bite my lip. "You're very bossy when you're holding a camera," I say. "And, in the bedroom."

"Because I'm in control. Are you complaining?"

I shake my head.

"Good. Now, bottoms off and lay down."

My stomach somersaults as I do what he says and when I lay back, Nick steps up onto the bed. He positions a corner of the sheet over my lower body and starts snapping pictures from above, hovering over me, tilting the camera. "Stretch your arms above your head. Now turn."

Even though he's not even touching me, the situation is beyond erotic. He sets a foot on either side of me, trapping me between his long legs, and clicks away. I'm trying to concentrate, but the way he hovers over me, silver eyes hot, begins to make me want more.

I want him on top of me. I'm going to have to distract him somehow and cut this photo shoot short.

I wrap my hands around his ankles, writhe back and forth, finding the light and my best angles. Nick watches me closely and I see a muscle twitch in his cheek. When I drag myself up, wrap my arms around his leg and crush my breasts against his calf, looking up with what I hope is a seductive look, he hisses in a breath.

"Perfect," Nick rasps. "You're so damn gorgeous." He reaches down, pulls the sheet out of the way and turns my lower body one way and my upper body the other way. "Twist, baby."

Click, click, click.

"Yes, Daddy," I say with a wink.

When he groans and sets the camera on the nightstand, I know the photo shoot is over. But, I'm feeling bold. Nick is always in control and I want to see him relinquish the reins over to me for once. I think he's taught me well so far and now I want to test out what I've learned.

It's time for the student to seduce the teacher.

As he moves in, I slide back against the pile of pillows. "Take your clothes off," I say using his line on him.

Nick arches a dark brow and pauses, as though he's considering my words. "Alright," he concedes and stands up. He yanks his t-shirt off then slides his board shorts off. When he's standing there in front of me, so naked and aroused, my nerves slip a bit.

But, I'm not going to chicken out and I run through everything Jasmine said earlier. Very slowly, I crawl over to him and nod toward the chair in the corner. "Go sit."

"What if I don't want to sit?" he asks, a challenging gleam in his eyes.

"Oh, you do. Trust me." Again, I point to the chair. "I'm waiting."

"Aren't you saucy tonight?"

"You have no idea," I say and slide off the bed. When he finally sits down in the chair, I sashay over and move between his legs. Then, I lean down, place my hands on his muscular thighs and begin to trail my tongue over his chest, letting my long hair drag over his lap and tickle him.

His head drops back and, for a moment, he lets me have my way. But, then, he tries to regain control and wraps his hands around my wrists, tugging me forward to straddle him.

"Not yet," I whisper. When he reluctantly lets go, I resume kissing my way down his taut abs. Then, I slowly kneel between his legs, reach out and wrap my fingers around his long, hard length. I look up at him from beneath my lashes and see him struggling to keep it together. "I'm going to put you in my mouth," I tell him.

He lets out a ragged breath and grips the arm rests hard enough to turn his knuckles white.

I'm nervous and keep in mind all the little tricks Jasmine just shared: *Drag your hair over his lap. Watch your teeth. Use your tongue. Maintain eye contact. Suck til your cheeks cave in. And, don't ignore the jewels.*

I grip his smooth cock in my hand, wrap my lips around him and begin to pull him further into my mouth. Back and forth. All the way to the back of my throat.

"Fuck," he hisses.

And, for God's sake, don't gag. Just swallow and do it with a smile on your face.

No, I'm not going to gag. But, I am going to suck him until I see him lose control. I must be doing something right, because Nick slides his fingers through my hair and pulls. "Jesus…Christ…" he moans.

Then, his hips surge up and, all the while, he watches me, eyes silver and intense.

And, then he's gone. I can see the passion-glazed look that overtakes him and any semblance of control he was managing to hang onto disintegrates.

"Sav," he pants, thrusting his hips. "I'm going to come." He tries to pull me up, tugging on my hair, but I'm going to see this through.

I'm going to watch Nick surrender to me completely.

I suck harder and with a long, low groan, Nick's lower body jerks and shudders. When his hot liquid hits the back of my throat, I swallow it down like a pro.

I did it, I think, and pull back, strangely proud of myself. I've never done that before and I think I just rocked his world. It takes him a few moments to get himself together and I climb up onto his lap and kiss him thoroughly. Making him taste himself.

Just like he did to me.

"Are you okay?" I ask, a twinkle in my eye.

His breathing has finally slowed down and he tightens his arms around me. "You're really something else. You know that?" he asks, his voice full of wonder.

"And, don't you forget it," I whisper.

Chapter Sixteen: Nick

While I wait to meet with my lawyer the next day, I can't stop thinking about Savannah and how our little photo shoot last night turned into the best blow job of my life. *Christ.* That girl goes from saint to temptress faster than my Dodge Demon goes from zero to sixty.

I squeeze my eyes shut and an image of her mouth gliding up and down my cock pops into my mind. I let out a harsh breath and move the magazine I'm pretending to read over to cover my lap better.

Yeah, my cock remembers last night damn well.

I broke another rule, I realize, but, fuck, it was worth it. Letting her take control resulted in a mind-blowing orgasm that I felt all the way to the depths of my soul. *Maybe it's time to amend the always be in charge rule,* I think.

Here's the thing, though. I had already broken one rule with Savannah by crossing that professional line. Hell, crossing it? We soared past it by about a million miles. And, now, I'm feeling things that I've never felt before about a woman.

Fuck. That means I'm on the verge of breaking my last rule. I'm trying to keep things purely physical, but I realize that I've developed more than just affection for her. Granted, she's my wife, but it doesn't matter. My dad destroyed my mom when he cheated and left.

People, including and probably especially spouses, pick up and leave all the time. Other halves who thought they were in a loving and committed relationship are left blindsided and devastated, trying to pick up the broken pieces of their heart.

I refuse to set myself up for that.

But, I can't deny it. I'm getting more attached than I'd like. And, that scares the shit out of me.

Savannah is young, beautiful and on the verge of fame. Everyone is going to want a piece of her. What if she wakes up one day while in some exotic location and wonders why the hell she married me? She'll meet someone more her age, have crazy sex with him and send me divorce papers.

My heart clenches.

I'm going to do everything in my power to avoid that. I have to be able to walk away because there comes a day when every love story ends, right?

Love. *Fuck. You're not in love, Nick.* You're only in lust. Savannah is a young, hot piece of ass who just happens to be sweet, innocent and your wife.

But, that doesn't mean I'm going to be stupid and fall in love with her. That would be the kiss of death.

"Nick? How are you?"

I stand up and shake my lawyer's hand. "Good, thanks, Lance. How about you?"

"I've been better," he says, a distant look in his eye. "C'mon into my office."

Lance Erickson has been a friend for years, though we don't see each other as often as we'd like with our busy schedules. "Sorry to hear that," I say and follow him.

"Yeah, well, my bitch of a wife just filed for divorce." He motions to the chairs in front of his desk. "Have a seat."

See, a little voice says. *It never lasts.*

"Shit, I'm sorry." I sit down, my mind instantly turning to Savannah.

"Ten years in the toilet. I heard she's shacking up with some guy from her office."

"Damn. That's harsh." I don't know what else to say.

"But, congratulations on your marriage," he says and manages a half-smile. "I wish you better luck than I had."

"Thanks," I mumble.

"At least you're able to finally cash in now and get that inheritance. I honestly wasn't sure you'd ever marry Margo, but I wish you the best."

"Um, I didn't marry Margo."

He raises a surprised brow. "I didn't know you started dating anyone new."

"Yeah, well, it's, ah, an interesting story," I say and shift in my seat.

"Well, shit, now you have to tell me," Lance says and leans forward. "Guess love makes people do crazy things."

I glance down at the open folder where there's a bunch of paperwork that I need to sign in order to get my inheritance.

This is the real reason you married Savannah, I tell myself. It has to be because anything else is unthinkable. Utterly ridiculous.

Because I refuse to believe love has anything to do with it.

Nick Knight does not believe in love, I remind myself. *So, snap the fuck out of it.*

When I get back to Sunset Terrace, I hear the shower flip off and I take the folder from Lance with copies of everything I just signed and stick it in my duffle bag. The money should be transferred over by 5pm tonight.

It's a relief. I can pay off some of the bills that have been suffocating me and maybe buy something nice for Savannah. We still need to pick out rings, but, for some reason, I'm reluctant to bring it up. It's almost like it's still not real right now. But, the moment we each wear a band around our finger, there's no denying it.

I head back up the hall and the bathroom door opens. I freeze when Savannah steps out, towel wrapped around her, in a cloud of steam. At the tempting sight, hot steam seems to rise in me, too, scorching my blood.

"Hi," she says.

I pull her into my arms and kiss her, moving my lips over hers leisurely, completely familiar now with every soft curve and corner of her mouth. She returns the kiss enthusiastically like always then pulls back. She lays a hand on my chest and gives me that loaded smile that's part angel, part devil.

God, it turns me on. When I slide my hands up under the towel, she giggles and pulls away. "I have some news," she says. "My parents and sister are coming out to visit."

I force a smile. "Great." I'm not looking forward to meeting her parents, especially her father. What if he hates me? I know that sounds a little irrational, but fathers never seem to like me. They always give me this look like they wish I'd just shrivel up and disappear. Or, drop dead.

"They should be here in a couple hours."

I blink in complete surprise. "They're coming now? Today?"

She nods and gives me a huge smile. "I can't wait for you to meet them. They're staying at a hotel up the street. We're meeting them tonight for dinner, okay?"

"Sure," I say.

Oh, great. I was hoping to put this off for maybe a couple more months, but I guess they'd want to meet their daughter's new husband sooner than later.

"Anything I should know?" I ask, trying not to let myself feel nervous.

"Just that they're going to love you," she says, tilts her head up and kisses my jaw.

Love me? Ha. Savannah did not prepare me for the third-degree that was her father. After she introduced us and we all sat down, the interrogation began. They all had a million questions and that's to be expected, I suppose, but I would've guessed Bob Hart was a retired military officer, not a school teacher.

And, he held nothing back.

"I just don't understand who in their right mind gets married after 24 hours? And, in Vegas? How drunk were you two?"

"Dad," Savannah says. "We had our reasons and…"

And, what? Everyone waits for her to continue, but what is there to say? Hell, we didn't really even have an answer why we did it. I mean, I wanted to collect my inheritance, but Savannah didn't get anything out of our arrangement.

Except me. And, let's face it, I'm not the greatest catch. I'm moody, grumpy, bossy, difficult-

"Nick is perfect for me," Savannah says, breaking into my thoughts. "We complement each other."

We do? Yeah, I guess we do. She definitely has a way of bringing out my better side. Truthfully, I've never been so happy.

"So, what's the deal? You couldn't find someone your own age, Nick?"

I clear my throat, not quite sure what to say to that.

"Dad!" Savannah says and her younger sister Bri stifles a giggle while her mom chokes on her wine mid-sip.

"I know there's a bit of an age difference-" I begin, but then get interrupted.

"Just a bit," Bob says in a dry voice and takes a long drink of his beer.

Be polite, Nick, I remind myself. "But, I guess when you know, you know."

Cindy, Savannah's mom, smiles. She's more easygoing than her husband and doesn't seem upset about our sudden marriage at all. "Honey, cut them some slack. They're in love."

My gaze snaps up to Savannah's and I feel panic move through me. But, just for a split second. Her steady, blue eyes settle me and a calmness fills me. People keep bringing up the "L" word and it's insane. We aren't in love.

We're screwing like bunnies and having a damn good time doing it. But, we barely know each other.

Shit. That's not exactly true anymore and I can't keep using that excuse forever. Because I actually know quite a bit about Savannah Marie Hart-Knight. Especially because we talk for hours every night and play that little game she calls "Questions & Secrets."

I know her favorite color is blue. But, not just any shade of blue. It's that deep, bright midnight blue that lasts less than a minute right after dusk and just before full night hits. I know when she gets nervous, she starts to pick at her nail polish. Like she's doing right now. I know she likes when I comfort her so I reach over into her lap and take her hand in mine.

I know that she likes to read before bedtime-- mostly horror novels which makes me laugh because then she drifts off to sleep like she's been reading a romance instead of about a serial killer. But, she never has nightmares. She prefers scary movies over rom-coms and Liam Hemsworth over his overrated brother. She doesn't care much about clothes or fashion for being a model and would much rather be in comfy leggings and a t-shirt.

Lately, she's been wearing my t-shirts a lot. She says they smell like me, apparently citrusy, and she likes that.

And, I know how she tastes. So sweet. Just like a bowl of freshly-washed berries in June. She smells like sugar-dipped jasmine and, right before she comes, I know that her bright blue eyes darken a shade from aqua to teal.

Ah, damn, I've learned more about Savannah in a couple of weeks than I ever cared to learn about Margo in a year. Maybe I am falling for my wife. A little, anyway.

Fuck it. A lot, okay? I'm falling for her a lot. And, God help me, I'm falling hard and fast.

I left for two hours this morning to settle the paperwork with Lance and I missed her.

So much for my rules. I've ignored every last one.

Who am I?

"A man in love is a force to reckon with," Cindy says.

"I think it's romantic," Bri says. "I'm happy for you, Savvy. And, I'm glad you're a part of our family, Nick."

"Thanks, Bri," I say.

As the waiter sets our dinners in front of us, I look over at her father. I may not have gotten his approval yet, but the Hart women love me. I see her dad say something to the waiter and with a nod, he leaves.

While we eat, Cindy and Bri start asking more questions about where we're living and what it's like in Malibu.

"We're not at the beach house right now," I say, "but when we get back, you'll all have to visit."

Bri squeals. "I can't believe you're going to be living right on the ocean. Do you ever see dolphins?" she asks.

I nod. "All the time. But, a couple of times a year, big groups of bottle-nosed dolphins migrate past my place and I'll go out there and swim with them."

"Seriously? That's so cool." Bri's eyes widen. They're more green than Savannah's blue and she seems to possess a more outgoing personality than her sister. Sav told me she's involved in every group at school, has a ton of friends and I'm not surprised.

By the time dinner ends, I feel better. Bob let up on the probing questions and snarky comments and we've been laughing and sharing stories for almost 40 minutes now. After clearing the dishes away, the waiter brings five glasses and a bottle of champagne to the table. He pops the cork, fills our glasses and Bob lifts his in a toast.

"Despite how quickly this all happened, I want nothing but the best for you both. So, cheers to a long and happy marriage."

We all clink glasses and, as I sip my champagne, I look over the rim at Savannah whose entire face seems to glow. When she winks at me, I know that I passed the test and have her family's approval.

I'm not sure why it's so important to me, but it is, and I couldn't be happier.

Chapter Seventeen: Savannah

The next couple of days, I enjoy hanging out with my family, and Nick and I take them all around town and out to eat. It's cute to see how they're all warming up to him so fast. It's almost like the moody man I met that first night at Beauty & Essex was a completely different person.

He's more affectionate than he's ever been and I love it when he grabs my hand and twines his fingers through mine. Or, when he drops a kiss on my head for no apparent reason. I'm still not sure where his heart is or if it's even involved at this point. But, I'd like to believe it is and that maybe he's developing feelings for me like I have for him.

Even though we can sit there and talk for hours, he hasn't said anything about love. I haven't either, and a part of me really wants to let him know how I'm feeling. But, I'm not going to lie. It's really scary. The last thing I want is to look like a foolish, little girl. Until Nick, I'd never been in love, not even close.

There's no mistaking this overwhelming feeling, though. I want to be near him constantly and when we're apart, even for a short time, I miss him. Every time he walks into the room, my heart beats faster. I love everything about him-- the way he looks, smells, tastes. Everything physical from how tall he is to his dark hair to the way his gray eyes melt into hot silver before he kisses me.

But, even more so, I love the way he treats me with so much care and respect. He may be a little bossy in the bedroom and on set, but he always makes sure I'm taken care of whether we're out somewhere or just sitting at home. I never would've thought he could be so thoughtful. He makes me feel safe and loved.

A big part of me is contemplating turning down the job in Capri. Nick mentioned retiring early from modeling and I've been thinking about it more and more. I know that I don't have enough yet to finish school and open a practice, but if I keep modeling, I won't be able to spend as much time with Nick.

And, right now, there's nothing that I want more. He's infiltrated my life, every single one of my thoughts and turned me into a woman who wants to spend the majority of her time with her husband. I don't think there's anything too wrong with that. Especially since we're still learning about each other and figuring out how to make this work.

My parents and sister leave the next afternoon and when we return from dropping them off at the airport, Nick tells me he wants to head over to the gym for a couple of hours.

"Wanna come?"

"Yes," I say in a low voice and trail my finger up his arm. "But, I'm not referring to the gym."

Nick lets out a low growl and drags me into his arms. God, every time he kisses me, I melt. I open my mouth, inviting his tongue inside, and meet it with a welcoming suck. With a half-laugh he pulls back and eyes me. "You are not the same girl you were two weeks ago."

"That's an understatement."

"As much as I'd like to scoop you up and have my way with you, I need to go workout. Otherwise, after all the eating we've done the last few days, I'm going to get flabby."

"I doubt that," I say and run my hand down his deliciously tight abs.

He grabs my hand, pulls it up to his lips and places an open-mouthed kiss in my palm. His eyes never leave mine and, as he finishes the kiss, I take a finger and slip it between his lips. I can see his eyes widen a little in surprise, but he must like it because he sucks my finger into his mouth before releasing it.

"You're a tease," he says, voice husky.

"Oh, I'm not teasing you, Nick. You can have whatever you want. Whenever you want."

For a moment, I think he's going to grab me and drag me into the bedroom, but then he regains his control. "Hold that thought, sweetheart," he says. "I'll be back in an hour."

"I thought you said two hours?"

"*One* hour. And, when I get back, I expect you to be waiting in bed. Naked."

"I don't know if I can't wait that long," I say, dragging my towel up a little, hoping to make him regret leaving. "I may have to start pleasuring myself while I wait."

Silver fire flashes in his eyes. "Goddammit," he swears and yanks me against his body. He kisses me hard, threads his fingers through my hair and pulls my head back so he can stare into my eyes. "Don't touch yourself until I get back."

"Why? You want to watch?" I ask, feeling extremely naughty. I like this newfound power I hold over him. He desires me and it feels so damn good.

He sucks in a breath and presses another hard kiss to my mouth. As he pulls back, he nips my lower lip. "You're damn right I want to watch."

A slow, wicked smile curves my mouth. "Tick-tock, Daddy," I purr.

Again, he looks on the verge of changing his mind, like he might rip off my towel and drag me down to the floor. But, then, he seems to be considering something and sticks with his original plan. "Be back soon," he says.

I give him a pouty look and shoo him away. "Go work out your perfect body. If you're lucky, I'll be here waiting."

He narrows his eyes. "Naked."

I roll my eyes. "We'll see," I say and squeal when he pinches my ass on the way past.

"*Naked*," he says again.

After Nick leaves, I get dressed, clean up the apartment and decide to make dinner for us tonight. I pull out the paper where his mom wrote down the recipe for his favorite macaroni and cheese and read it over. Then, I look through the fridge and cupboards to see if we have everything I need. Looks like it, but I don't have bread crumbs. I suppose I could make some, but I'm hardly known for my cooking skills.

So, I pick up my phone and call his mom. "Hi, Judy, it's Savannah," I say when she answers.

"Hi, honey. How are you?"

I really like his mom. Both Judy and Bob, actually. They gave me a much easier time than my dad gave Nick, but I suppose that's because he still thinks of me as his little girl.

"I'm going to make the mac and cheese, but don't have breadcrumbs." I pull a loaf of bread off the top of the microwave. "Can you tell me how to make homemade ones? I've got a loaf of bread here."

"Of course. It's very easy and homemade will taste better, anyway."

Thirty minutes later, I don't just like his mom. I *adore* her. She not only walked me through making the recipe until I placed the casserole dish in the oven, but also talked with me like I've been her daughter-in-law for years.

As I set the timer on the oven, I figure I still have about ten minutes before I'm supposed to be naked in bed. Boy, is he something, I think with a smirk.

"I should probably get going," I say. "Thank you so much for helping me."

"Oh, anytime, honey. I'm so glad you called. Oh, and I meant to ask if Nick received the inheritance yet?"

My ears perk up. "Inheritance?"

"You know, from his Grandma. We weren't ever sure he'd actually get it," she says with a chuckle. "But, Lena was pretty firm about him finding love and being married first. Personally, I think she was just scared he'd wind up having a midlife crisis and blow it on some big, crazy purchase like a boat or fancy car or something."

"Right," I laugh, playing along. *What is she talking about?*

"Alright, well, have a good night and let's talk soon."

"Sounds good. Bye, Judy."

I mull over what she just said about an inheritance from his Grandma. Nick never mentioned a word about it so I'm a little confused. The way she made it sound…

No. I shake my head, not letting my thoughts stray that way. But now I'm beyond curious. I'm not sure what I'm looking for, but I wander into my bedroom and my gaze drops to his duffel bag laying in the corner. It's open and I move closer.

I am not a snoop. Not usually, anyway. I glance at the clock on my nightstand and know that he's going to be home any minute now. So, I have to move fast. I drop down and reach into his bag, shift a few things over and feel a folder.

With a frown, I pull it out and see what looks like a law firm's name and logo on the front. A bad feeling curls in the pit of my stomach and I almost put it back. Except, I want to know if the small, niggling suspicion at the back of my mind is right.

I hope to God it isn't.

I open the folder and scan down the first page. It's a lot of lawyer mumbo-jumbo, but when I get to the part about Nicholas Knight, Grandson of Lena Eleanor Maxwell, and her leaving him two-hundred thousand dollars, my eyes widen. Then, the following sentence hits me like a dagger to the heart. *"...contingent on his decision to enter matrimony..."*

My mouth drops open and I re-read the entire paragraph three times. And, with every word, my heart sinks further and further in despair.

Oh, my God. Nick married me to get his inheritance.

I feel like such a complete fool. Here I am in a bubble of hearts and flowers, believing that I'm in love with a man who is obviously only using me. I was on the verge of passing on the career opportunity of a lifetime because I didn't want it to take time away from Nick.

How could I have been so naive? So trusting? So fucking stupid?

I am so furious with myself and Nick that I can't even see straight. He never mentioned one word about this so I know he didn't want me to find out. If he had developed any true feelings for me then he would've told me about this.

But, he kept it a secret and used me. Why else would he want to elope in Vegas after being an asshole to me then doing a complete one-eighty switch and pretending he's into me? God, it all makes sense now. His motive was so despicable, so dishonorable, and I feel beyond betrayed.

He never cared for me. It was all an act and I fell for it hook, line and sinker. He stole my innocence, whispered pretty lies to me and then cashed his inheritance check. I drop down on the bed and run my hands through my long hair.

Nick Knight is a fucking asshole. A liar who made me believe that he actually cared.

And, I fell in love with him.

Tears prick my eyes and when I hear the front door open, I swipe them away. No, I refuse to let him see me cry. I won't give him the satisfaction. When he steps into the bedroom, I can't even look at him.

"You don't look nak-" His voice abruptly cuts off and drops down to the folder laying on the bed next to me.

I finally muster the courage to look up at him. "How could you?" I ask.

"Savannah, it's not what you think," he says. A flicker of panic passes through his gray eyes, but then it's gone.

"Then, please, explain this," I say. I'm pissed and I know I probably shouldn't do it, but I grab the folder, stand up and throw it at him. The papers fly everywhere and his eyes narrow.

"I know this looks bad-" he begins.

"Bad?" I repeat. "It looks worse than bad. Did you get me drunk and convince me to marry you so you could get your hands on this money?"

"If I remember correctly, it didn't take much convincing," he says, voice turning cool.

"That's not the point. Why did you dare me to marry you, Nick? Tell me, dammit. Just for once be honest and stop lying to me," I yell.

His face goes completely blank. "I never lied to you, Savannah."

"You've been using me this whole time!"

Nick lets out a frustrated sigh. "Okay, yes, maybe I should've told you about the clause and the money. But, honestly, I didn't do anything about it until this morning. I've been too busy getting to know you these past couple of weeks."

"Oh, because it slipped your mind? You forgot about $200 grand?"

"I didn't say that. Don't put words in my mouth."

My chest is heaving up and down hard and I'm so upset my hands are shaking. I clench them into fists and grind my jaw. "Just tell me," I say in a harsh whisper.

He shifts and glares down at the folder on the floor. "Why were you going through my shit?"

Oh, no, he's not about to turn this around and make me look like the one at fault. "Your mom told me. She must've just assumed it was important enough for my husband to share. And, your stupid bag was open."

"I was going to tell you…"

Sure, I think. "You are so full of it. The only reason you married me was so you could claim your inheritance. Please, stop insulting my intelligence by trying to convince me that you actually care."

There. I just set it all up for him. Now is his chance to convince me that he does care. To pull me into his arms and tell me that it's not about the money anymore. That somewhere on this crazy journey, he fell in love with me and money, be damned. The only thing he wants in his life is me now and forever.

Say it, Nick.

I'm holding my breath. Waiting, hoping, praying for him to tell me what I so desperately want to hear.

But, he doesn't say a damn thing. Just looks at me with that cool, unreadable expression. In fact, he barely looks upset. He may as well have just stabbed me in the heart. I'd rather have him yelling at me and showing some kind of emotion than just standing there looking so unflappable.

I walk over, pull my hand back and crack him across his face. "You're a bastard," I hiss.

He moves his jaw back and forth then looks at me with insouciant gray eyes. "I know," he says.

All of the air leaves my lungs and I want to curl up and cry. But, not yet. Not in front of Nick. "Go," I say and point to the front door. "Just leave. I can't even look at you."

Nick bends over, scoops the paperwork up, grabs his duffel bag and heads for the door.

He's not even going to try to apologize, I realize. I follow him down the hall, in a daze, but I have nothing left to say.

Nick reaches for the handle, opens the door and pauses. Then, he glances over his shoulder. "For what it's worth, I broke all of my rules for you."

I frown and have no idea what he's talking about. And, before I can ask, Nick walks out, and that traitor Paul follows, right on his heels.

The moment the door closes, I collapse down onto the floor and cry my eyes out. I've never felt so utterly devastated.

Chapter Eighteen: Nick

As I drive back to my place in Malibu, I'm still in a state of shock and trying to understand what the hell just happened. My mom may have let it slip about the inheritance, but it was my responsibility to tell Savannah. This is all my fault. I should've told her about the money the minute it stopped mattering.

Because it did.

The money took a backseat to her and all of the feelings she's been stirring up inside of me. At some point on this insane journey, I fell in love with her.

It's the only explanation for why I'm so upset right now.

The only reason you married me was so you could claim your inheritance. Please, stop insulting my intelligence by trying to convince me that you actually care.

I do care. I care so fucking much and I have no idea what to do now.

Back at the beach house, Paul and I walk down the shoreline and all I can think about is the hurt on Savannah's face. I handled the situation all wrong and instead of fighting for her, I walked away.

I've never had to fight for anyone in my life, I realize. Women always fawned over me, sought me out. When it came to sex and relationships, I guess I've put in minimal effort. Until Savannah.

Why did you dare me to marry you, Nick? Tell me, dammit.

But, I couldn't. I froze up and the words stuck in my throat, refusing to come out.

Again, I ponder over her question. The question that I've been asking myself since that night in Vegas, but haven't quite had an answer to until now. Yes, I chalked up the quickie marriage to wanting my inheritance. But, I always knew in the back of my mind that there was more to it.

And, now I know.

The moment I laid eyes on Savannah Hart at the restaurant, I felt my heart beat again. It had stopped years earlier when I saw my dad break my poor mom's heart. He literally destroyed her by leaving her for another woman. All of my beliefs in love, marriage and romance dried up and scattered in the wind when I walked in on my mom, curled up on the bed, sobbing her eyes out. "Don't ever fall in love," she had whispered. "If things don't work out, it'll destroy you."

I never forgot that and vowed to follow her advice. Even after she found love again with John, I still kept my walls up and never allowed any woman to get beyond them. When my modeling career launched into the stratosphere at 18, I made up the first two rules that I've followed for nearly the past 25 years: Never get emotionally-involved and keep it purely physical because it's imperative to be able to walk away and not look back. And, always call the shots, especially in bed, because relinquishing control leads to vulnerability.

Then, when I began working behind the camera, I made my third rule which is to not mix business with pleasure and never sleep with the models.

By following my rules, I closed myself off to hurt. I guess I also closed myself off to living. And, most assuredly, to love. And, then, Savannah came into my life with her bright blue eyes and shy smile. She was a breath of fresh air and she intrigued me. When pushing her away didn't work, I tried the opposite approach.

And, wound up married 24 hours later.

She snuck up on me like a thief in the night, stealing my cold heart and warming it up to feelings again. To the point where now I can't walk away. She also managed to usurp control in my life and in the bedroom.

Now, I'm exposed and powerless.

Ironically, I don't regret a thing. Except for not being able to communicate my thoughts and feelings to her earlier. It's so hard for me, though, because this is all new and unexpected. "Shit," I say and shove a hand through my hair. I toss the ball and Paul races after it, kicking up wet sand. It's time to explain everything to Savannah even though it means opening myself up to rejection and heartbreak. The very things I've gone out of my way to avoid my entire life.

Sonofabitch.

It's not going to be easy. I'm going to have to gather my thoughts and practice because if I don't get the words out perfectly, she may decide this whole thing was just a mistake and it's better to move on than waste more time with my emotionally-stunted ass.

"Paul!" I clap my hands and whistle and he runs back, ball in his mouth. "C'mon, buddy. We need to come up with a damn good speech to get your Momma back."

Paul gives a woof.

Back at the beach house, I sit on the couch with a beer, Paul at my feet chewing a bone, and realize how empty it feels without Savannah and her vivacious presence. She lights up the room and now that she's not here, it just seems dark and cold. But, I'm not going to waste time being depressed. This isn't over yet. I'm going to fight for my girl.

I spend the next three hours drinking and writing my thoughts down in a notebook. It's extremely important to me that this apology is perfect. I need her to understand me and forgive me. When I finally think I've poured out every single thought in my head, I lift the notebook and focus on Paul. "Paul," I say. The dog is half asleep, but manages to open sleepy eyes and look up at me. "I need to practice, okay? Do me a favor and listen to my groveling."

I take a deep breath and gaze into Paul's big, brown eyes. But, I'm picturing Savannah's bright blue ones. "First, I want to say I'm sorry for walking out last night. I should've stayed and tried to talk things through, but I'm not the best at communicating my feelings. I'm working on it, though."

Paul gives a snort and lays all the way down. God, the dog doesn't even believe me.

"Sav, I need you to know how much I've come to care about you. I can't imagine living without you. You bring so much to my life and I'm sorry for being a jerk…"

I sigh and finish my beer. I hope I sound genuine, but I think it sounds borderline pathetic. When I look back down at the 20 pages I filled in the notebook, front and back, my handwriting begins to look blurry. I rub my fists into my grainy eyes and yawn. Six empty beer bottles sit on the coffee table in front of me and my watch reads 3am. Guess I should call it a night.

Because first thing tomorrow, I'm heading over to Sunset Terrace to win my wife back.

Unfortunately, things don't go how I plan in the morning. After waking up extra early, jogging down the beach with Paul, showering and downing a quick cup of coffee, I practice my speech again. It takes me 20 minutes to get the whole thing out and just as I finish up, there's a knock on the door.

Savannah, I think, and my heart jolts against my ribs. Paul jumps up and barks.

I jog over, throw the door open and see Margo. *Dammit.*

"Margo, I was just about to leave-"

Margo sweeps right past me and I roll my eyes. "Where's your child bride?" she asks in a haughty voice.

"Savannah isn't here." Paul growls low in the back of his throat and I pet his head. "Easy boy."

She glances down at Paul and makes a face at the dog. "Did she leave you already, Nicholas?"

My eyes narrow and I cross my arms. "What do you want? Did you come to pay for the window you broke?"

Margo raises a slim brow, but neither confirms or denies anything about breaking my window. She does look pleased, though, as she glances around the room. Probably because there's absolutely no sign that Savannah ever lived here. "I've decided to give you another chance," she announces.

What? Is she delusional? "I'm married, Margo."

She laughs. "It was a quickie, tacky Vegas wedding. I have no idea what you were thinking, but I came here to tell you that once you get your head screwed on straight again and get this marriage annulled, we can start over."

"I'd have to get a divorce and that's not going to happen."

"What in the world can you possibly have in common with someone who is half your age?"

"I don't know how to explain this kindly so I'll just lay it out there: I never loved you, Margo, so why would I want to get back together with you?"

"You're an idiot, Nick. Who said anything about love? Marriage to me comes with half a billion dollars and social prestige. That used to mean something to you."

I just shake my head. "Not anymore."

"Oh, so you think you're better than me now?"

"No, I don't."

"Then, what's your problem?"

"No problem. I just finally fell in love."

My admission seems to shock her into a moment of silence. "Wow. I'm sure you think that now, but you're not in love. You're not capable of love. I remember how cool you can be. How you can turn your emotions on and off. Don't fool yourself. People like us-- we don't fall in love. It's a weakness."

"I used to think that. But, not anymore."

Margo lets out an annoyed sigh. "You've seriously lost your mind."

But, I shake my head. "No. I think for the first time in my life, I'm thinking clearly. And, I need to leave so if you're finished..."

Her pale green eyes shoot flames and Margo looks ready to murder me. "When she leaves you, don't you dare come back to me. Because she will, you know. It's only a matter of time. Your precious Savannah is going to leave just like your father did."

Her words hit me hard and then she sweeps out. What if Margo is right? What if Savannah doesn't want to hear me out? What if-

No. I'm going to make her listen. I know she cares.

She has to care. I refuse to believe I'm in this marriage all by myself.

When I reach Sunset Terrace, it's quiet and I take a deep breath and knock on Savannah's door. I probably should have texted her first, but I need to talk to her in person.

"She's not there," a deep voice says.

I turn and see Ryan Fox. He holds a metal toolbox and looks like he's been doing some repairs around the complex. "Did she run out? Do you know when she'll be back?"

Ryan suddenly looks uncomfortable and shifts the toolbox to his other hand. "I don't know what exactly happened between the two of you, Nick, but when I saw Savannah leave earlier this morning, she looked really upset."

"Leave?" I ask and frown.

Ryan looks like he's debating whether or not to say more. He sighs. "For Capri. I figured you knew."

I can't believe she just left and didn't tell me. Why would she not at least let me know?

Because she doesn't care, a small voice says. *She thinks you're an asshole and she's done with you.*

"Fuck," I hiss out and lean over, hands on my knees. I feel like I'm going to puke. I stand back up and suddenly have no idea what to say or do. I feel like the only good thing in my life is gone. And, I was such a complete idiot for throwing away all of my rules and believing it could work.

"Do you want to sit down? Have a drink or something?" Ryan looks concerned, but I just shake my head.

Then, I turn and walk away.

Back at the beach house, I sit on the balcony, downing Jack Daniels and scrolling through my camera, looking at all of the pictures I've taken of Savannah. I start at the beginning with the Vegas shoot. Day one, she looked like an angel and I was so awful to her because she made me feel things that I didn't want to admit. That I was scared to explore.

When I come to the picture I secretly took of her, with the wind blowing the gauzy dress up and the blazing blue sky and mountains behind her, my heart clenches. Actually, I think it just shattered.

I pour more whiskey into my glass and down it. All I want to do is numb the pain, but it's not fucking working. I start scanning through the pictures again. Day two was brilliant. My sexy, sweet little temptress looks at me with a come-hither smile that hovers at the edge of her red lips.

I forward through the rest of the Guess shoot and then stop. I've reached the shots we took on the Fourth of July. That night after the barbecue where I told her to take her bikini off. *Christ, talk about fireworks.* I can't stop from looking at them. They're tasteful, beautiful and so fucking hot that I instantly get hard.

I've never been so goddamn miserable in my life. These pictures should be on display at some gallery somewhere. Their beauty should be shared and appreciated. But, I would never let anyone else see them. These tantalizing images are all mine and no one else's. Mine to enjoy, savor and jack off to, I decide.

I set my camera aside and drop my head back. My mom was right. If it doesn't work out with the person you love, that love has the power to turn around and destroy you.

The idea that Savannah and I are over leaves me distraught. I can't even process it.

Because if I do, I'm terrified that it will completely break me.

Chapter Nineteen: Savannah

Capri is absolutely breathtaking. The island, located in Italy's Bay of Naples, has a rugged landscape, upscale hotels and a cove-studded coastline full of floating yachts. This should be the most exciting trip of my life, but I can't seem to enjoy any of it.

All I can do is think about Nick.

I haven't heard a word from him since he left my apartment that night after I confronted him about his inheritance. Not a call, not a text, nothing. His silence is louder than anything he could say, though.

It's quite clear that he is done with me. Done with our marriage. He got what he wanted so what else is there?

I just don't understand how he was capable of turning so cold, so fast. I don't think I've stopped crying since I left L.A. and arrived here. And, now, I'm supposed to go on the biggest job of my career and pose with Simon LaFleur, the top male model in the world, when all I want to do is crawl into my bed and continue sobbing my eyes out.

I know I look terrible with puffy eyes and dark circles. I've lost weight and that's not good because it makes me look skeletal. God, they're probably going to think I'm a heroin addict or something. The makeup team definitely has their work cut out for them.

When I arrive on set, it's a stunning spot, with rocky cliffs and bright blue sea. And, I instantly think of Nick. I can only imagine the shots he would be able to capture here. But, no, Nick's gone. He doesn't need me anymore. Doesn't want me anymore.

The crew greets me warmly, but it's pretty clear something is wrong with me. My normal friendliness and constant smile is long-gone and sadness emanates from every pore. I can't even hide it.

Veronica, the photographer, is already there and greets me enthusiastically. She starts going over her vision and I nod numbly. Then, a car pulls up and everyone watches Simon LaFleur get out. He's about 6'2" with a slim build and Golden Boy good looks.

Simon heads over to us and embraces Veronica. I guess they worked together before. Then, he turns those emerald green eyes on me and grabs me in a huge hug, too. "Bonjour ma beauté," Simon says in a French accent. "It's so nice to finally be able to work with you, Savannah. I've been looking forward to it."

I force a smile. "Thank you. That's sweet." I remember Nick telling me what a player Simon is so I don't want to encourage him too much by being over-friendly. But, really what does it matter? Maybe flirting with Simon will help me feel better. Force me to get over Nick.

Yeah, right. That's just wishful thinking on my part. I don't think I'm ever going to be able to get over Nick Knight. He's a part of my soul now.

"You two are going to look amazing together," Veronica says, looking us both over closely. "With your similar coloring and complementary features…" She gives a little victory punch in the air. "I have a feeling this shoot is going to be epic."

"Yes," Simon practically purrs and leans into me. "I have a very good feeling, too."

Ugh. We've been together for two minutes and he's already trying to get into my pants. I can feel it in the way he looks at me and it's starting to make me uncomfortable. If he tries anything, I'm just going to have to be clear with him that I'm not interested and that I have a husband. Even though my husband wants nothing to do with me, Simon doesn't need to know that.

After the usual couple of hours getting hair, makeup and wardrobe done, Veronica motions us over to the edge of the sea where there's a huge cluster of rocks. Every so often the waves hit and the ocean sprays up into the air. She'll probably be able to get some good shots if she times it just right, but I have a feeling I'm about to get soaked.

Veronica tells us to climb up onto the rocks and I study the tall, jagged boulders warily. I'm wearing crazy tall heels and the last thing I want to do is slip and fall. I take a step up and when I wobble, Simon reaches down and offers a hand.

"Come on, grab on. I've got you, ma chérie."

Without much of an option, I grab his hand and he lifts me up onto the top of the rock beside him. Veronica tells me to lay on my back and she wants Simon on top of me. We're supposed to gaze into each other's eyes like we're in love.

I suppress a sigh and lay down. The hard slab is uneven and jagged and presses into my back making it almost painful. I try to get more comfortable, but then Simon drops down and stretches over me, pushing me even harder into the rocks.

Suck it up, Savvy. Every photo shoot isn't going to be a pleasure cruise. This is work, an amazing job you're lucky to have, and you're getting paid a ridiculous amount of money to be in Capri and work with a gorgeous man and talented photographer.

I keep repeating this mantra, hoping it will help turn my attitude around. Because I am grateful for the opportunity. I just can't keep my head straight and I find myself thinking back to the Vegas shoot.

Nick started off like the biggest jerk in the world, but I couldn't get over how attractive he looked sitting at the bar at Beauty & Essex, sipping his Jack on the rocks. There was something about him that drew me in and made me want to get to know him better. He intrigued me like no other man ever had before.

After he apologized on set and invited me to dinner at the Stratosphere, I remained wary, but still interested. He was so much fun that night. There's no one else I would've wanted to run all over the city with and act so silly.

We drank, danced, kissed, played and got married.

That was the best night of my life and, even though I'm sad now, I wouldn't change a thing.

"Savannah! Head up!"

When I hear Veronica's direction, I snap back to the present and try to focus. I know I'm doing a half-ass job and that's not good. I don't want to mess up this opportunity or the client's campaign so I give myself a mental shake and look up into Simon's green eyes.

"All good?" he asks.

I nod even though his heavy body is grinding my back into the jagged rocks.

"Wave incoming!" Veronica yells. "Make sure to straighten that leg, Savannah. Here it comes in three, two, one!"

I straighten my leg out, arch my back and gaze up at Simon with what I hope looks like complete infatuation. The ocean shoots up behind us and a wall of sea spray drops and covers us with a salty mist.

We both laugh and I try to blink past the burning in my eyes. Ten waves later, I can't see at all and my eyes are on fire from the salt water. Simon is facing down so it isn't affecting him nearly as much. He sees that I'm having a rough time, but he doesn't look too concerned. He's more worried about making sure the sun hits his face just right.

I tilt my head toward Veronica. "Can we take a break?" I ask.

"Can you hang in there for a few more waves?" she asks. "I almost have the shot I want."

Oh, for God's sake. Nick would've gotten the shot on the first take. I clench my teeth and hope I don't end up going blind. Finally, after what feels like bloody forever, Simon rolls off me and I sit up. Everything hurts-- my eyes, my back, my butt, my legs. Simon pops up and scales down the rocks with ease, but I have these blasted heels on so I'm forced to slide down which sucks for the back of my thighs and ass.

I think I scrape half my skin off on the way down and I'm starting to get pissed. I don't mean to act like a diva, but this is ridiculous. I yank the heels off and stomp over to the craft service tent where I grab a water and dab at my eyes.

"Holy shit, Savannah," JoJo, the makeup artist, exclaims. "Your back is all jacked up. C'mere, darlin', and let's put some ice on it."

I glance over where Veronica and Simon are talking and narrow my eyes. This isn't going how I would've hoped. Obviously, my gloomy thoughts started the downward spiral, but now I think I have a pretty good right to be ticked off.

But, I've always prided myself in being a teamplayer. A model who is easygoing and tries hard to do her best at all times. I don't like drama and I've never been one to make waves.

I've also never been treated like this. Is my bad mood just turning me into a big cry baby?

I flinch when JoJo presses a bag of ice against my back left shoulder. "That water washed away half your eye makeup," she grumbles and shakes her head. "What an asinine shot to make you do."

"Thanks, JoJo," I say.

I wish I could say the rest of the day gets better, but it doesn't. Simon is a complete and total narcissist who only cares about how he looks in each shot. He constantly blocks my light and makes sure he's in the better position. By the end of the day, I don't even care anymore.

Maybe Nick was right when he tossed out the idea of retiring from modeling and starting vet school. Ultimately, it's what I want to do. It's my dream. Modeling used to be a fun way to make money, but maybe when you hit a certain point, the fun goes away.

Because what I'm doing right now isn't fun. I'd much rather be curled up on the couch next to Nick reading thick textbooks about the anatomy and physiology of animals.

Nick…

God, I can't stop thinking about him. A part of me wants to go back to the hotel and text or call him. But, what in the world would I say?

There's really nothing to say.

Except maybe I love you.

Yeah, right. I'd rather fall off that big rock and drown in the sea than admit that to Nick. He told me without hesitation that he doesn't believe in love. That life isn't a fairytale.

Love isn't for me...I don't fall in love, Savannah.

If only I thought there was a chance. Even a small one, I'd reach out to him.

But, who am I kidding? Nick made his feelings quite clear.

When we finally wrap for the day, I'm mentally and physically exhausted. Back at the hotel, I pin my hair up, get undressed and take a long soak in the bathtub. I'm stiff and sore so it does wonders. Afterward, as I slip my robe on, there's a knock at the door.

I'm not expecting anyone, but maybe it's Veronica. She was probably thoroughly unimpressed with my modeling today and wants to make sure I'll be better tomorrow. I definitely could use a pep talk, I think, and open the door.

But, it's not Veronica. It's Simon and he waltzes right in without being invited.

"Bonsoir, ma chérie," he says. "I just wanted to check in. You seemed-- how do you say it? Not all present today?"

"Off my game?" I suggest.

"Oui, exactement."

"I just have a lot of things on my mind," I say.

He sidles up to me and runs a hand up my arm. "Perhaps we can find something to do to help you relax and forget your worries, no?"

"I'm married," I blurt out.

He shrugs. "No matter. Everyone takes a lover while on location."

My eyes widen. "Well, I don't."

"You're far too uptight, ma chérie. Why don't you let me help you relax?"

When he grabs my upper arms and pulls me forward, I twist away. "Don't touch me, Simon!"

"Come now, don't be so rigid."

"Get away from her," a deep voice orders.

Heart in my throat, I look around Simon and see Nick standing in the doorway. A silver hellfire burns in his eyes and suddenly I feel bad for poor Simon.

I have a feeling if he doesn't bolt right now, Nick is going to kick his scrawny ass from one side of Capri to the other.

Chapter Twenty: Nick

I am about ready to kick this punk's ass. I try to keep my shit together, but the image of his hands on her, grabbing her when she clearly said no, pushes me over the edge. I take a step forward, hands clenched into fists, and Simon immediately releases Savannah.

Fear flashes through his eyes and he backs away, hands up, palms facing out. "I don't want any trouble," he says.

Something dark and angry propels me forward and I'm ready to drop this asshole with a punch. Simon must see the bloodlust in my eyes because he skirts around me and takes off. I fake like I'm going to grab him and he gives a little cry.

Guess the pretty boy doesn't want to get his face messed up.

After Simon disappears, I turn back to Savannah. I feel my heart give a kick and realize just how much I've missed her.

I'm going to get you back, sweetheart.

"What are you doing here?" she asks.

"I've been doing a lot of thinking since I last saw you," I say.

"And?"

I suck in a deep breath. *Here goes nothing.* "And, I miss you so damn much it hurts." Her face shifts from completely blank to a look that strikes me as hopeful. I think, anyway. "I've never been very good at opening myself up, but before you kick me out, I hope you'll listen to what I came here to say."

She gives a small nod and I take a step closer.

"I never meant to hurt you, Savannah. I know I should've told you about the inheritance sooner than later, but I was scared it would change things."

"What do you mean?" she asks.

"When you married me, you had no idea about the money. Yet, you still said yes." I study her closely, my gaze fastened to her beautiful aqua eyes. "Why?"

"I already told you, Nick. Because I had a glimpse of the inside."

"What do you mean?"

"Even though you were a complete jerk to me, I saw your inner beauty when you sat down in the dirt next to a stray dog. I watched when you gave him food and water, talked to him and rubbed his belly. Only a very kind person would do that."

For a moment, I don't know what to say. "Anybody would've done that."

"No, everyone else ignored him. But, you didn't. You paid your assistant to get him cleaned up and back to L.A. where you gave him a home."

Her words make me feel a little self-conscious and I shift my weight from one foot to the other. "He misses you, you know."

"Who? You or Paul?"

"Both of us."

Savannah pulls her robe tighter, watching me closely.

"Savannah, when I dared you to marry me, I tried to convince myself it was because of the money, but that isn't totally true. It's because...you brought me back to life." I let out a sigh and scratch my fingers through my hair. "I don't ever talk about when my dad left my mom. It broke her and it took a very long time for her to find happiness again. It's not something that I ever forgot and I always swore to protect myself from that kind of heartbreak. That's why I never let myself get emotionally-involved with women. But, you changed all that, Sav. You have this enthusiasm and brightness that surrounds you. It drew me to you and made me want to take a chance."

"Nick-"

I hear the uncertainty in her voice and I can't bear the idea that she doesn't want me back. "Wait. There's more." I lift the curled-up notebook that I've been wringing and twisting since sitting at the airport this morning. "Sorry, I'm not very good at this so I wrote it all down."

When I offer her the notebook, she looks at it and, for a heartbeat, I'm not sure she's going to take it. But, then her hand reaches out and her slim fingers wrap around it. "What exactly did you write down?" she asks and uncurls it. She flips through the pages.

"What I'm feeling, I guess. I started with 20 pages and I think I hit about 50 on the plane ride over. Front and back," I add.

She looks up and I see that bright light surrounding her that made me fall for her on day one. "That's very sweet. No one ever wrote 100 pages for me about how they feel."

When she gives me a little smile, I want to grab her and pull her into my arms. But, I have a feeling I'm not out of the woods quite yet. "You're the best thing that ever happened to me, Savannah. You wanted to know why I asked you to marry me," I say. "Well, the night we met, my heart beat again. I know that probably sounds stupid, but it's the best way I can explain it. How you made me feel, I mean."

"It's not stupid, Nick. It's actually kind of adorable."

"Yeah?" I ask and feel my mouth edge up in the first smile I've felt in days.

"Yeah," she says and moves closer to me. When she's directly in front of me, Savannah lays a hand on the left side of my chest. "And, what's your heart feeling now?"

A very strong emotion swells within me and it can only be one thing. "Love," I admit in a low voice. A sheen of tears fills her eyes and when one slips free and slides down her cheek, I brush it away. "I love you, Savannah. I did from the very beginning. I was just too stubborn to realize it."

When she smiles, I pull her into my arms and capture her lips in a slow, tender kiss. She leans into me and returns the kiss with such a sweetness that something inside me fractures. But, it's a good break, though. The kind that makes the rest of my walls come tumbling down.

After a long moment, we pull apart. "You've turned me into a sap, you know that?" I say and kiss the tip of her nose.

"I'm glad," she says and walks her fingers up my chest. "Because I want to hear you say it again."

"I love you," I tell her. Then, I pick her up and spin her around until she squeals.

"Good because I love you, too. So, so much," she tells me, blue eyes shining.

I kiss her again and hear her stomach growl.

"I've been so upset, I haven't eaten in days," she admits with a sheepish look.

"You look too thin. C'mon, let's go get some food into you."

After Savannah slips into a sundress and sandals, we leave the hotel and wander down the street. We end up finding a quaint, little restaurant a few minutes away and I order almost everything on the menu for her. It's far too much food, but I don't care because she needs to eat.

The meal is delicious and, after they clear the numerous dishes away, we sip limoncello and gaze out at the sea as the sun sets. The stunning explosion of reds and oranges makes the sky look like its afire.

Everything is beautiful once again, I think, and look over at my girl.

Now that Savannah is back, my world feels right again.

I reach over and lace my fingers through hers and just savor the warm breeze on my face and the feel of her hand in mine. *God, I love this woman.*

"Can I ask you something?

I look over at her and feel this warmth spread through me. "You can ask me anything, sweetheart."

"What did you mean when you said you broke all of your rules for me?"

I tense up a little and don't want to think about when we were fighting. But, I'm not going to keep things from her anymore. "I used to have three unbreakable rules that I followed. 'Til you, anyway," I add.

"Tell me."

"Are you sure you want to hear? They might remind you of what an idiot I used to be." When she nods, I take a deep breath and then tell her.

After a moment, she tilts her head as though considering them. "I'm not surprised by one and three. But, you never let a woman take control in bed? Hmm. We may have to work on that one."

"If I remember correctly," I say in a low voice, "you sure took control after our little photo shoot."

Savannah smiles, pulls her hand out of mine and reaches for her glass. After she finishes the limoncello, her hand disappears beneath the table and slides over my upper thigh. Hidden beneath the tablecloth, her hand continues up and I suck in a sharp breath when it covers the front of my zipper.

"I think I'm going to take control more often, Nick. So, I hope that's okay?" she adds, all innocence.

I grit my jaw and manage a sharp nod. *Fuck.* When she squeezes, I shove my chair back, drop some money on the table and hurry her toward the exit. Once we're out the door, Savannah bursts into a fit of giggles

"I hope you know you're playing with fire right now."

"Well, then let's cool you off," she says and tugs me onto a shadowed pathway. She guides me down between some trees and then around a huge sea cliff.

When our feet hit the sand, I look up at the midnight sky and smile. "Your favorite color," I say.

"You remembered," she says with a smile and kicks her sandals off. Then, before I can say another word, she pulls her dress up over her head and tosses it on a rock. I feel a wall of heat slam into me as she shimmies out of her undergarments and stands there naked in the glow of moonlight. "Are you going to join me?" she asks.

But, I can't find my voice. So, instead, I just watch her sashay down to the sea and my mouth waters. I start to unbutton my shirt and glance around to make sure we're alone. The small cove is very private and the only sound around us is the constant lapping of the waves along the shore. I yank my pants and boxer briefs off and then step into the cool ocean.

Savannah watches me, water up to her shoulders, as I make my way closer. A few feet away, I dive under and swim beneath the surface until I reach her. I grab her leg and pop back up. She splashes me and laughs and I sweep her up, twirling us around. Her legs wrap around my waist and I slide my hands up under her, drop my head forward and kiss her.

It doesn't take long for the kiss to deepen and grow hotter. Savannah writhes against me and I lift her hips, rubbing against her center. I trail my lips down her neck, lost in the feel and taste of her. "God, I've missed you," I whisper and lick along her salty collarbone.

When I reach a hand down between us and stroke between her folds, she arches against my palm and lets out that throaty mewl that drives me crazy. "Please," she murmurs.

"Whatever you want, sweetheart. It's all yours."

When her hand wraps around my cock, I grasp her hips and line her up. Then, I pull her down and bury myself in the hilt. "Oh, God, Nick," she moans and grinds herself against me. I thrust up into her as the waves roll by us and plunge my tongue deep into her mouth.

Our bodies find a rhythm and it's desperate and hard. We missed each other too damn much and it's like we can't get enough.

It doesn't take long before our breathy cries are echoing across the water and then our orgasms hit at the exact same moment. I rip my mouth free and look deep into her eyes the moment I come inside her. My entire body trembles and those blue eyes of hers widen, her lips part as she cries out and her sweet body releases in a series of tremors.

Savannah gasps and drops against me and, I'm not going to lie, I nearly fall over from the sheer, fucking pleasure of it all. "Jesus," I hiss and tighten my arms around her, trying to find my balance.

When she finally lifts her head, I kiss her temple. "Lay back," I say. Savannah stretches back onto the surface, long legs still wrapped around me and floats. Her eyes close, her blonde hair drifts all around her and I've never seen anything more beautiful. She looks like some kind of sea nymph or siren come to tempt me from the depths of the ocean.

"You're too goddamn beautiful," I murmur, admiring the view of her slim body all stretched out before me, rising and falling with the waves. Water droplets roll off her curves and I lean down and suck a taut nipple into my mouth, laving and worshipping her breast until she's moaning again.

When I notice the goosebumps prickling her skin, I pull her back up, wrap my arms around her and start back toward the shore. I'm trying not to think too hard about the fact that we just had sex without protection. Instead, I enjoy the feel of her wet, slippery skin against mine.

Though it may have started off in fear and uncertainty, my trip to Capri is turning into everything I had hoped for and more.

"I love you, Sav," I whisper and hug her tightly to me.

"Nick…" she purrs and leans back to look up at me, moonlight splashed across her face. "I think I loved you the moment you first kissed me in Vegas."

My heart expands, threatening to burst from my chest, and I dip my head and kiss her salty lips again and again.

Epilogue: Savannah

After Nick shows up at my hotel room and then visits set every day for the next two weeks, Simon LaFleur becomes the perfect gentleman. He treats me with respect and no longer tries to dominate the photos, hog the lighting or intimidate me.

Under Nick's close watch, I blossom and, other than Las Vegas with Nick shooting me, I give the best poses of my career. Veronica and Guess are thrilled. After wrapping, Nick and I linger in Capri a few more days and enjoy each other's company. We also take another midnight swim in our cove.

Life couldn't be better.

When we finally arrive back in the States, Nick drives us to Sunset Terrace and I give Ryan Fox my notice. It's bittersweet because I will miss the girls, especially Jasmine, but there's a beach house in Malibu that's calling me home.

Nick and I pack all of my things up in boxes. I really didn't think I had that much until it's time to move it all. Then, it seems like a crapload of junk and I begin questioning whether I need the majority of it. But, Nick tells me to take it all and I can always sort through it later.

On my last night at Sunset Terrace, we have a barbecue and pool party. We drink and eat too much, splash and play in the pool and then sit around the firepit and talk until it's late. I'm really looking forward to living with Nick and Paul, but a part of me is sad that Jazz, Morgan and Taylor won't still be my neighbors.

"Don't look so sad," Taylor says and gives me another hug goodbye. "It's not like you're moving back to Ohio."

"I know," I say and swipe at my eyes. "I'm just being silly."

"You're going to be living on the beach!" Morgan says.

"And, we will come visit y'all a lot," Jasmine adds with a smile.

"You're welcome anytime," Nick says.

"Thanks for everything, you guys," I say and, after another round of hugs, I climb into the car with Nick and we go home.

Living in Malibu with Nick is everything I could have ever wanted. We stay up late watching scary movies or talking or making love. And, we sleep in every morning. Or, until Paul whines to be let outside.

I love sitting next to Nick on the balcony, drinking coffee in the morning and looking out over the ocean. There's something so pleasant and soothing about living on the water. The smell of sea salt in the air, the sound of the waves and the feel of the warm breeze through my hair and on my skin spoils me.

Nick spoils me, too. Especially when we drive over to a jeweler in Beverly Hills to pick out our rings. He opts for a plain silver band, but insists on getting the date we married in Las Vegas engraved on the inside curve.

Our anniversary, I think, and decide to do the same thing on my matching silver band.

When it comes to choosing an engagement ring, I don't need anything too extravagant, but Nick studies all of the diamond rings in the case and then chooses three. "If we did this the traditional way, I would have chosen one of these for you," he says.

They're all beautiful and way too expensive, I'm sure. But, my eye is drawn to the classic, round diamond that seems to sparkle brighter than the others. When he notices, Nick picks it up and slides it onto my finger. "This is the one," he says.

I couldn't agree more.

As the weeks fly by, neither of us is in a hurry to get back to work. Nor do we really need to and, honestly, all we want to do is spend time with each other. My last two campaigns alone will cover all of my schooling and then some. The more I think about it, the more my mind is made up, and I tell Nick that I'm going to retire from modeling.

"Are you sure?" he asks. "I don't want you to have any regrets."

We're standing on the beach, throwing the ball for Paul, and I shake my head. "As much as I enjoyed modeling, it's a big commitment and right now I have other things to focus on," I say and give him a mysterious smile.

"What kinds of things?" he asks and reaches out to take my hands in his.

As he pulls me closer, I pretend to think. "Well, I want to focus on being a good student," I say.

"Uh-huh," he murmurs and places a kiss on my cheekbone.

"And, of course, a good wife…"

"Oh, definitely," he agrees and drops a couple of kisses along my jawline.

"And, a good mother," I finish.

He pulls back and blinks as though he didn't quite hear me right. "Mother?" he repeats.

I nod and squeeze his hands. "I'm seven weeks pregnant."

It takes a moment for the words to register but, the moment they do, Nick looks at me in amazement. "You're sure?" he asks.

"Yep," I say with a smile.

"Oh, my God, Sav," he whispers and pulls me into his arms.

"I know it's probably sooner than we planned, but-"

"I'm going to be a Dad?" he asks, voice full of disbelief.

"Is that okay? I know the last time we talked about this, you kind of freaked out."

His silvery gaze holds mine and his smile makes my heart sing. "I don't think I've ever been happier. Well, except maybe that night in Capri…" he adds with a wicked smile.

"Most likely when the babies were conceived," I say.

He freezes. "*Babies?*"

I nod. "Yeah, remember when I told you how twins run in my family?"

For a moment, he looks like a deer caught in headlights, but then he reaches a hand out and touches my stomach. "Two?"

The wonder in his voice makes me smile and I lay my hand over his, holding it against my belly. "Go big or go home, right?"

"That's right," he says and chuckles.

I lift my hands and cup his face. "You are like no one I have ever met, Nicholas Knight. From driving me crazy until I wanted to walk off set before I murdered you to sweeping me off my feet and proposing marriage, I never knew what to expect."

"I'll tell you what you can expect, sweetheart," he says. "Expect me to love you for the rest of your life because I am never letting you go."

"I'm damn glad we stuck it out because you are the love of my life," I tell him. "And, I have a feeling our adventure is just beginning."

I pull Nick's dear face down and kiss him with all of the love and passion that's flowing through me. When Paul runs up and gives a whoof of approval, we both burst out laughing.

"Two?" he asks again.

"Two," I confirm.

He nods, warming up to the idea. "Probably both girls, huh?"

"Probably," I say.

"I hope they look just like you," he murmurs.

Then, Nick takes my hand in his and the three of us walk down the beach together.

Wait, no, I think, with a little smile. Make that the *five* of us.

Printed in Great Britain
by Amazon